<u>The Culminate Amethyst</u>
Ryan Keith Johnson

"The Culminate Amethyst"
Copy Right © 2007, 2012 and 2019
All rights reserved.
Red and Blue Dragon Fantasy LLC. and Lightning Source.
Cover Design by Ryan Keith Johnson
Photo taken by Dan Grevas
Sales tax included.

ISBN: 978-1-7339815-1-4

Other books

"The King's Retribution"
"Lion Ascend"
"What I Think About You: Song Lyrics and Poetry"
"The Temple of the Incubus"
"Red and Blue Dragon Fantasy Legacy Anthology
of Compositions and Short Short Stories"
"Blue Dragon Fantasy: Faded Memories and Short Stories"
"Red Dragon Fantasy: Song Lyrics and Poetry"
"An Angel's Whisper"

Animus stepped out of the forest after the last drop of rain, the sun revealed itself from behind the clouds and shined. The sunlight hit the grass while the rain drops of cloudburst fell upon them from the trees. Today was the day Animus would be with Princess Aarilinus and nothing was going to stop him, not even getting his feet wet from walking in the grass.

Animus was a young man, no older than eighteen, with shoulder length blonde hair and blue eyes. He was about six foot and one-hundred and sixty pounds with a small bone frame. He was the oldest of seven siblings who worked hard on the farm to help his father provide. Animus felt his life had no meaning because he was a peasant and was discriminated by the nobles' children and the nobles themselves. He was sad for a long time until he met Princess Aarilinus.

The peasant felt his heart beat faster when he saw her because he was in love. Some would argue that love at first sight makes time stand still. Except for Animus she was the missing puzzle piece in his life since he met her as a child. The princess

Ryan Keith Johnson

encouraged Animus to think positive about his life because looking ahead to your dreams is worth living for.

Animus dreamed of wearing the silk shirts and gold rings that nobles wore because he wanted to be rich. He wanted to sit in the luxurious carriages, eat exquisite meals and have live entertainment. For now, he would have to accept life as a farmer

The farm boy touched his black, cotton, vest while crossing his arms and remembered what grandfather told him before passing away. Grandpa, told him; be careful what you wish for, for you may get it.

The peasant walked near the cavern and the first gate to the castle until he heard the sound of metal moving together in a diabolical motion. Quickly, he jumped into a wagon full of hay that was nearby when he saw the guards walking towards him. Animus covered himself with the straw, as he realized that if he was found he would be put in the dungeons. After the guards walked past, talking amongst themselves, Animus unraveled himself from the pile of straw in the wagon. He ran his fingers through his hair to pull out the rest of the debris and looked around to see the soldiers continue to walk away.

Animus touched his cheek with his hands while staring at the towers and thought about how he was going to get up to her window. He could see the Mid Tower, which was Princess Aarilinus' bedroom and was surrounded by a big vine. Animus walked through the doors of the first gate which had serfs farming the land for the king and small townships around the first wall. He marched on the street to the entrance of the second gate or the second wall, which was a gate protecting the city, parks, libraries and universities as well as upper class living that surrounded the castle. Animus avoided the knights and soldiers by hiding behind wagons, horses and trees until he was in front of the Mid Tower, on the castle grounds. There was a brick wall dividing the castle from the city and a golden gate entrance that was open for the solders to march through which Animus walked through.

The dark green stalk was twisted around the tower like a snake as though it was protecting the princess. Animus felt his heart beat faster and knew that this was his last obstacle.

Animus knew that if the king caught him he would be imprisoned or worse put to death. King Owen was the sixth descendant of his family who had ruled Aria in times of peace. He was a middle aged king who was arrogant, protective but controlling. Animus remembered when he asked his father about King Owen and was told not bring it up because his father did not want his son to know about the past.

Animus wondered why Aria was so different than the neighboring kingdoms. He remembered what the elders said about Aria becoming a rogue nation and that the other kingdoms were likely going to attack to steal the riches. Animus asked the elders about Princess Aarilinus and was told that she was unlike any girl in the land.

The peasant gripped the dangling vine which felt like rope. He remembered the times he climbed up before and the consequences.

He pulled himself up with his arms and started climbing. His legs swung up against the brick wall and he gripped the vine while pulling himself up. The journey took most of the morning, but he managed to hold on until he reached another vine to continue onward. He swung himself to the stalk of a bigger vine and took a break to catch his breath as he saw the window sill. Animus rode the vine to the opening and he quickly grabbed the window sill. He held on to the edge of the wooden platform and pulled himself up, but didn't climb over the bottom part of the window. .

"Come to me, my sweet princess," said Animus.

An exquisite shadow emanated from the darkness, in the form of a young lady. Animus smiled as he remembered her qualities. Her gold belt shined over her red satin dress and her white skin was soft and complemented her soul. It reminded Animus of the porcelain dolls that were in the shops; all dressed well with their hair curly, long eye lashes and white skin.

Princess Aarilinus smiled at Animus as he did and she was happy to see him. Animus could see her hair was down and the wind slowly blew it back. Parts of her black hair stretched past her chest to her navel. When the wind stopped her bangs draped past her eyes to her chin.

"Animus is that you?" she asked and continued to smile.

"Yes, help me into your room so that I may tell you something," replied Animus.   "Tell me something?" began the princes. "Why don't you just tell me?"

"Please help me in, I can't hold on much longer," he begged.

Princess Aarilinus leaned over the window sill while she was on her elbows. Her hands clasped together on top of the smooth textured wooden ledge, "you know father would skin you alive if he ever found out you were in my room, alone with me."

"Your father would not let me hang here, begging for help. He would strike a dagger through my heart and watch me fall."

Princess Aarilinus smiled and covered her mouth to keep from laughing, "if father found out how long we've been seeing each other he would skin us both."

The princess burst into laughter and helped Animus inside her room. She admired and loved him for the man he was, but she didn't want him to be caught by father, "you shouldn't be here. You know that he's going to kill you."

"Not now or ever again, your father will listen and accept my proposal to marry you," replied Animus with a serious attitude.

"You must stop risking your life to see me," the princess replied with a raised eyebrow.

"What heart can resist your beauty and love as much as mine?" asked Animus.

"Father insists I should marry someone of royalty. No matter how much I refuse and speak of choosing you he insists that because I am a princess I should marry a prince and not a peasant," she answered.

"What if there is a way for us to be together?" said Animus as he slowly put his hands on her abdomen and held her close, with her face up to his.

"I don't understand?" she asked

"Aarilina, I am a prince."

She put her arms around Animus' shoulders and looked at him as she smiled. She was an elegant young lady that had a small bone frame and was five inches shorter than him. Her lips embraced his with a kiss as she remembered when they met as children for what seemed like ages ago.

"What am I going to do with you?" she whispered.

"Run away with me," he replied with a smile.

Princess Aarilinus was quiet and looked into his blue eyes as she thought about how beautiful he was inside. He was a man deemed worthy of cherishing, but with no place to go.

"Tell me you love me and I will run away with you," she said.

"Lets get started with our life together," insisted Animus.

"How do you know everything will be ok?" she asked.

"I've heard the news yesterday that your father has involved a mask to be the treasure that is to be retrieved for your hand."

"A mask? What power would my father dream of having now?" she sighed.

"It grants the possessor magic powers," replied Animus.

"If my father had such a jewel there would be no telling what he would do," whispered Aarilina as her eyes looked away and he let her go.

She turned away frightened at the idea of what power would do to her father. Animus knew by the way she turned away that it was something she didn't want to face. The princess was strong, but the material world faced her like the sharp edge of a sword.

"I don't understand, what pertinence does it have for us?" she asked as her head turned halfway for Animus to see the side of her face and finally she turned completely away so he could only see her hair.

"He wants the mask and I want you," said Animus as he walked behind her and touched her arm. She hid her face that was full of emotions by remaining turned away and knew that she didn't want her father to be lost to greed.

Animus held the princess gently in his arms, with her back against his chest, and she closed her eyes as she felt his strength. Animus had his arms and hands around her chest while tickling the back of her neck with his lips. Then Aarilina realized she wouldn't have to face the unknown future alone.

There was a brief silence as Animus let the princess turn around to look into his eyes. It had been to long since he was exiled six months ago and Aarilina couldn't stand to lose him.

"Tell me this is not a dream," she whispered.

"A dream it is and you shall never wake up," replied Animus.

"Do you promise we'll always be together?" she asked.

"I give you my word," he answered.

A grin surfaced as she closed her eyes momentarily while she licked her lips to speak of activities that reached the mind of a girl. Suddenly, the sound of a fist hitting the door rattled the door hinges and Aarilina shot up from the bed with a gasp.

"Hide," she whispered as she turned around to face the door and tried to act natural.

Animus looked around the bedroom, realizing he was not in a dream at all, but in the Mid Tower. A dead end that meant hiding from the king would be like trying to escape from a tiger. The farm boy turned to Aarilina and saw a gesture from her eyes directing him to hide under her bed. Animus slipped under her bed and felt the smooth wooden floor against his back. It wasn't comfortable, but he was more concerned about not getting caught by the king. It had been a devastating situation six months ago since the last capture and he didn't want to be apprehended again. The only reason he was released was because he begged the king for his life and the king didn't know his last name or who his father was.

"Aarilina can I come in, please?" asked her father.

"What do you want?" she demanded while turning the door knob, letting a crack surface from the door. She didn't like the fact that father was invading her privacy and felt he was on to her love affair with Animus.

King Owen entered the room slowly, wearing his red robe and crown, as light from the window reached his green eyes. King Owen called her Aarilina also and she had no choice, but to allow it. No one else called her Aarilina except father and Animus.

King Owen was an old man balding on the top of his head with red hair, he had a strong build and a large bone frame. He was a few inches shorter than Animus and loved his daughter more than anything. He was frustrated with Aarilina because she was being stubborn and wanted the best for her as far as choosing the right man.

"Father, there is nothing to discuss," she replied and turned away to look out the window.

"I have granted the rights for the man to marry you after retrieving the mask of Furrengee. I have been making preparations for your survival," said King Owen.

"Survival from what father?" asked Aarilina.

"As princess you will marry an honorable suitor out of five and lead a life free of despair."

"Who are these suitors?" she asked turning around to face the king.

Princess Aarilinus felt used and wondered how she could trust him when he intended to use her to get what he wanted. She turned back around to the window and looked at the flowers that grew from the giant vine as soon as the anger heaved her stomach like a fireball. She heard the king move behind her from the sound of creaking floor boards and felt his hand touch her arm. His hands were cold like death, but tickled her insides as she remembered when he played with her as a little girl.

Princess Aarilinus turned from the window and looked into her father's eyes to see how cold they had become. She wondered what happened to him in the past that caused them to drift apart.

"These men will make you happy. They are Prince Tusk of Kalindor, Prince Corsair of Sporsindor, Prince Rubin of Endswood, Prince Domineer of Aryan and Prince Lordoriouse of Stalous. They are the five men I've selected to go on this quest and retrieve the mask of Furrengee."

"Are they young and handsome?" she spoke with raised eyebrows.

"They are very handsome indeed," he replied.

"Are they tall and bold?" Aarilina continued with the grace of such lips.

"They are very tall," King Owen continued.

"Are they strong, loving and able to hold my heart forever?" she asked.

"By what words would a prince be if he did not hold your heart with his?"

answered her father.

"What is the mask of Furrengee? What does it do?" she asked.

"They're retrieving a mask that was once worn by a great warrior who united the kingdoms as one against evil," said the king.

"I don't understand? What has this got to do with me? Father, I can't be forced to choose a man to be with, when I don't know him."

"Aarilina you must do this, for me and the people of Aria. You're the bridge stone to all that lies after me. The five men are strong , powerful and forth rite. They will protect you against any enemy that will come to destroy Aria. They will treat you right in a loving marriage," he said.

"Marriage?" asked Aarilina as she revealed a peculiar look.

"I would rather be a virgin than to do what you command of me," she began. "I choose a life of being myself with someone I love rather than living my life with expectation and sadness. The feeling of love is immortal and your meaning of marriage is hollow," she declared.

"How did you come to this conclusion when you've never been in love?" replied her father as he raised his eyebrows.

"I have my ways of discovery," began Princess Aarilinus.

"I've found my true consort and after the days passed I looked up the word. The stories read, the poetry recited, the songs sang and the feelings from memories. I know of the word as it knows me," she continued.

King Owen hesitated as he tried to think of who she was talking about and then lit up as he remembered, "if you're speaking of the peasant I banished from the kingdom, then think no more. The dreams you fantasize of having, in your reality, is poison and it will spread like a plague to the people who serve you and would follow you as a great leader."

"My love is poison or you?" asked the princess.

"I pity your fantasy to marry that peasant. When the people find out there king is a low life like your Animus they will turn against you and your stupid escapade. Aria will fall and you will find your neck stretched on the edge of a guillotine," declared King Owen.

Aarilina was quiet as her lips trembled and with a shakened voice she replied,

"when I become queen I will bring love, joy, and happiness, which is something you don't do. The people will love me and will die to protect me."

"Enough!" yelled the king.

Princess Aarilinus had her eyes closed expecting to get slapped, but there was nothing. She reopened them to find a cold stare from father and felt her nerves being pinched. Her father had never hit her and somehow knew that he never would but this time she wasn't sure.

"You're in love with him! A peasant, a farm boy, a rechid nobody with no past and no future. I made a mistake to allow this Animus to live instead of throwing him to the Dark Wolves," replied King Owen.

"Really, father you would kill a defenseless peasant for falling in love with me?"

"I will do whatever it takes to protect my lineage. Maybe you should explain;

why do you choose him?"

"If you must know, I choose him because he is the one," she raised her voice and continued, "Animus makes me happy when I'm sad and as his soul resonates with me, I feel special. I feel like the characters in the stories I've read from my favorite writers and play writes, Sancta Perlova, Avah Maria or Neva Ester. When I kiss him I feel myself float upon the air as a feather moves in the blowing wind."

Aarilina's eyes closed as she relived the memories of kissing Animus then she reopened them to see father's eyes protruding at her. King Owen's cheeks turned red as his right hand started fidgeting in outrage. She watched the king look away from her and as they looked on the floor she knew he was serious. Aarilina sensed jealousy from her father who didn't want to share her with any man he didn't think was good enough.

"You will marry whoever retrieves the mask of Furrengee and this man will be a prince not some poor beggar who lives in a mud hut," answered King Owen as he turned around and gave her a stern look before slamming the door to leave.

Aarilina took a deep breath; walked to the window and listened to the sound of sparrows chirping as well as looking at the beauty of the kingdom from where she stood. She wished things were simpler, easier, and less complicated, but it would never happen. Life was going to become difficult for her and she knew today was the beginning of it.

"You can come out now," she said while turning around from the window.

Animus slid out from under the bed and jumped to his feet. His eyes met with Aarilina's and they seemed troubled from the argument he witnessed. The peasant touched her soft, warm hand and watched the princess smile slowly. He wished he could be more to her than what he was now. He knew he wasn't a prince, he wasn't rich and all he had was his heart, but he knew it wasn't enough because she frowned again.

"Animus seek the mask," said Aarilina as she started to get emotional but kept herself calm.

"If there is a way you can change the laws of Aria then search it out," replied Animus.

"I can't, the laws have been like this since Aria came to order. Only a king can change the laws and I am only a princess."

"Go now and seek the mask before he finds out you were here," said the princess but got no response. "Animus please," she continued. "This isn't a game, this isn't funny."

"He is an arrogant, self-centered, egotistical pig and he will get what is coming to him," said Animus.

The words versed so easily that he didn't realize that words could carry. The green eye from outside the key hole opened wide then it protruded. It was King Owen eaves dropping on his daughter from outside her door. He had a feeling Animus was there and instead of breaking down the door he continued to listen.

"Why do you risk everything for this visit today?" asked Aarilina as she dried her eyes with her hand.

"What more would you have me do? If I lived another life, a new life as the elves, I would spin a web of dreams and cast you away from here," said Animus as he tried to cheer her up.

The princess took a deep breath to relieve herself from crying and began laughing. She liked the way he spoke to her in poetry because it helped her cope and discover answers to the problems in her life.

"If you could choose a different life, but keep your beauty what would it be?" asked Animus.

"I would trade all my power for the life of a peasant," she replied confidently.

"Then do so now," he whispered while touching her face.

Aarilina slowly grinned while looking into Animus' eyes and dreamed of the day of doing just that, living as a peasant girl in a small house on a farm where everything was simple. It seemed so easy in thought to just drop everything and run away. There was one problem, father would give into the hunt of a lifetime that would result in Animus' death and Aarilina being miserable again.

"Animus where would we go?" she asked.

"Far away, anywhere you want."

"I wish it was that easy, but our destiny is diverse in comparison that can't be changed by the course of the universe. You have chosen your destiny and that is to seek the mask. My destiny is for my people and I have felt it my whole life to give what Aria needs that has been forgotten and that is a good queen who is just a fair."

"I understand," replied Animus.

"Don't be troubled, my dear consort. After a pale moon becomes full and the land is covered in blue we shall come together," she declared with a smile.

"Someday?" asked Animus.

"One day," she replied.

"Then I will sail through the ocean and feel you blow my sails to safety. The mask of Furrengee shall be mine and I will use it to seek you out when I return to the castle," said Animus confidently.

"Then go now my prince for the time is young and I will wait until I am an old woman for your return," said Aarilina with a smile as she watched him walk to the window sill. He turned to look at her, smiled before climbing down the vine.

Through the spiraling staircase of the Mid Tower an old woman in her fifties named Jenna took each step nice and slow. She wore a long dark, green, dress and her eyes matched the dark brown hair that hung to the middle of her back in a braided ponytail. In a way, Jenna was a surrogate mother to Aarilina because she took care of her when she was a baby. They even looked alike and had the same relationship as a mother and daughter did. All of the handmaidens looked up to Jenna Cranston because she was the queen's most trusted handmaiden and devoted her life to serve the king and queen. She never married, she never fell deeply in love with a man to stay with and she never had children. Jenna's parents were merchants passing through and abandoned her at the castle to the old king and queen. Jenna heard from the handmaidens that the time for Aarilina to be given away was drawing near. The eldest handmaiden stepped slowly to each step to not fall down. When she got to the princess' door she looked up to see the king kneeled down in front of the key hole, "your highness."

King Owen had just heard Animus leave the room and shot up from kneeling in front of the door. He was embarrassed and at a loss for words because he was caught.

"I was, just examining the door handle and the key hole. I noticed that it's dirty with rust covering the metal."

"I would have our servants sand off the rust and polish the door," said Jenna.

"I was considering that option, thank you Jenna," stammered the king as he smiled.

"I'm sure you were," she answered with a joyous look.

"Great, what news do you bring for me?" asked King Owen.

"Well, I was going to tell the princess that Prince Tusk is coming to visit. He sent an emissary to let us know he was coming and he will be here in a few minutes. He's probably here now."

"I'll meet with him. Come, let's go together," smiled the king.

Animus' feet landed on the ground and he looked around for the king's soldiers. He smiled as he remembered what Aarilina said to him; *Then go now my prince for the time is young and I will wait as an old woman for your return.* It gave him a warm fuzzy feeling inside his abdomen and made him want to start his quest right away. He needed to talk to his father, Adam, to know more about the mask and where it was kept.

The peasant looked around to see there were no soldiers around and he took a deep breath and relaxed. The young man immediately walked quickly towards the golden gate with the castle behind him, to go out the way he came in.

Suddenly, he ran to hide behind the bushes when he heard the sound of a horse charging through the open golden gate and cobblestone path. A man in black armor riding a black stallion, followed by five guards on regular horses entered the front area of the castle.

The man got off his horse and the emissary bowed to the prince and he was greeted by an old maiden and King Owen who led the stranger into the castle. Animus watched through the bushes as he heard the name Prince Tusk of Kalindor. The other princes weren't going to attend until tomorrow. King Owen was going to make it difficult for him to retrieve the mask of Furrengee by sending men who could fight well to proclaim the mask for Aarilina's hand in marriage.

Princess Aarilinus was lying on the bed and was writing in her diary. She felt an inspiration today; one that would enable the birth of the next song that would be sung to Animus. Images fluttered through such mind of Animus and the feelings she had for him while she wrote the poem. The name of the composition was *Like Magic It Is*, which was short and small. Then there was a knock at the door that broke the girl's concentration.

"Who is it?" she asked.

"It's me," said a familiar voice.

"Father, what do you want?" she asked as she walked to the door.

"Prince Tusk of Kalindor is here and he would like to meet you," replied the king.

The door opened slowly as Aarilina's eyes looked at the man without his helmet, who was dressed in black armor. His eyes were brown with hair to match and a small patch of his bangs was white and he looked at her. Aarilina felt threatened by him because he was dressed in armor and wasn't dressed formally. She didn't know him, but she had a gut feeling that his interest in her was not intellect.

"I'm pleased to meet you, my lady," he kneeled down as he looked at her and reached for her hand to kiss it.

"As I am of you," Aarilina smiled as she gave him her hand and he kissed it.

"Well I'll leave you two alone. I have matters that need attending," replied the king.

"Father, surely you can take Prince Tusk with you so that I can continue my daily activities," said Aarilina in a stammer as he rose up and released her hand.

"Prince Tusk is our guest and I'm sure you can show him around before you resume your hobbies," said the king before he left.

Prince Tusk watched the king leave and when he was gone he looked at the princess, "I have wanted to meet you for a long time, I remember having dreams of you. We were married, happy and had many sons. The sun shined on your perspired body that later turned to diamonds," said prince Tusk.

"I had no idea that word of my beauty reached Kalindor," said the princess as she continued "I would imagine that I would be in most men's dreams as their lover."

"Oh, but every man in my kingdom wishes to get a glimpse of the princess of Aria," grinned Prince Tusk as he saw the piece of paper that was in her left hand. Then he looked up at her face, her beautiful face, then her neck. He saw the necklace around her neck with what looked like a red ruby.

"That's a nice necklace you're wearing. Is that a red amethyst with a gold chain ?" asked the prince as he got silence and disingenuous expression from the princess.

"What's this?" he asked and took the composition from her hand.

"If you must know I'm busy," she raised her voice while feeling irritated and took the paper back.

"You write poetry of love and magic what made you write this piece?" he asked.

"It's written beyond the bounds of our universe," she answered.

"Maybe you should sing it to me."

"The sound of my door closing will be the only singing you will hear."

"Who is your lover?" began Prince Tusk smiling in an antagonizing tone. "Why doesn't he come to meet the challenges of the mask? You kind of remind me of one of my peasants girl that I won in a sword match. She had a lot of fight in her, but after I broke her she does what I ask. Are you a lioness or are you a dog?"

"Nobody owns me," said Aarilina in anger.

"Anybody can be bought," smiled Prince Tusk.

"Men like you believe you can rule the world," said Princess Aarilinus as she stared into his eyes and continued. "I belong to no man, no matter how much father marvels your greatness I'll spit upon you as the scum of all insects and wipe my shoe of your every presence," she declared.

"Oooohh, you are cruel. All I asked was are you a lioness or a dog and you snap back like I am this terrible thing."

"Because you are," said the princess as she continued. "If you act like a monster then you are a monster."

"So if I am a monster then I am a good monster," he replied with a smile and continued. "Princess I shall proclaim the mask and own you like my black stallion," he smiled and licked his lips. "We don't live in a free world where you can choose who you want to be with. Kings need to control others so we don't have enemies controlling us."

Prince Tusk turned away from the princess who defied him. Never before had he met a woman who was this stubborn and rejected to be his subordinate. The prince ran his fingers through his hair and bristly chin as he tried to think of a way to shake things up. He insulted her and now he wanted to confuse her and when he got the mask he would brainwash her before breaking her like a horse.

"Forgive me your highness. I don't own you and I wouldn't choose to," he replied as he turned to face her before crying. "I don't know how to express how I feel through this thick armor that I wear as skin."

Princess Aarilinus mouth dropped as she watched the tears fall. Prince Tusk fell to his knees and cuddled to her feet.

"Your majesty," said the princess confused.

"I'm not perfect, I only come to express greatness and the will to share my heroic efforts with you. My biggest problem is that I have had no experience of love with women because I believed no woman would ever give me strength to believe in something so mighty!" he cried.

"Why do you think I'm great?" asked the princess as she looked uneasy.

"The strongest thing I heard about you is not only your beauty, but because you care about what happens to your people. That's something every prince can learn from," said Prince Tusk.

"Please your majesty, rise to your feet and dry your eyes. It's obvious we must learn from our mistakes," she replied.

He rose eye level to her, wiped his eyes and was about to kiss her until she raised her hand in front of him, "No man shall kiss me until he returns with mask."

"Very well," said the prince as he sniffled with a nod and left.

When the prince was gone. The princess was alone and confused because of the way he acted towards her. Was he genuine in his affection or was he using her? Or worse, was he crazy? Prince Tusk cried his tears to her, but did it mean that he would change for the better? Aarilina missed Animus touching her back and tickling her rib cage, but what she missed the most was Animus listening to her when she needed someone to talk to.

She smiled and thought about how romantic Animus was when he climbed up the tower to be with her, just as he had a few times earlier. The princess walked over to the window sill with the poem and started writing as she hummed to herself until she heard the sound of a new carriage and looked below.

The princess let out a sigh and thought of meeting a new prince who would prove why they should be together. All Aarilina needed was Animus; the very man she was forbidden to have.

The princess walked to her bed and set her poem aside to pull out her secret diary; with the stroke of her pen, she wrote the last thoughts of Prince Tusk. The creepy prince, who escaped the dark hole of craziness, the scary one who shot orders that was to be followed and then started crying to her royal feet when she retaliated. Before she reached the middle of the page to free her mind from the torment of a folly prince there was a pounding at the door. Aarilina jumped up from her bed and hid the diary between her bed sheets.

"Who is it?" she asked.

"It's your father, dear."

"Oh father, what news do you bring for me now?"

"It's a surprise my dear. Come, open the door so I can show you who wants to see you."

"Really," she said and hesitated as she tried to think. "Father I don't think I can take anymore surprises in one day. Prince Tusk has already taken quite a beating on my soul."

"As I understand it, he told me you two are a match made in heaven. Would you open the door please there's someone who wants to meet you," demanded the king.

The hinges began squeaking while the door opened a crack revealing the light from the window. Finally, the door opened all the way for the princess to reveal herself. She saw a man with father who was quite handsome with long hair. The prince was young, handsome and had sandy brown hair that stretched to the middle of his back. His smile revealed deep dimples along his high cheek bones. His bangs were bushy and over his eyebrows. His large build could be seen though his dark red silky shirt and blue pants.

"This is Prince Domineer; I have a meeting with Prince Tusk, enjoy each others company," replied King Owen before he left.

Aarilina walked back in her room as Domineer followed and could feel him looking at her body.

"So, Prince Domineer, tell me about yourself? When you become king what do you plan to do for your kingdom?" she asked before turning around and looked into his blue eyes.

"I like to spend the day creating plans for the peasants in Aryan, trading with other kingdoms for livestock, food and treasures. I like to go out exploring other lands, going on treasure hunts and discovering waterfalls from far away lands."

"Well it sounds like every woman desires you," smiled Aarilina.

"Yes, I enjoy the nights with the selected handmaiden's back home. I believe, as king, I should have the power to choose whoever and how many women I deem worthy to have a lustful night with," said Prince Domineer in a serious tone as his eyes looked deep into Aarilina's eyes, not realizing he offended her.

The princess slowly shook her head back and forth as the prince looked at her confused and asked her, "what's the matter?"

"Why would one woman choose a pig such as yourself and find you share the bed with multiple women?" she asked.

"I'm sorry, but as king I have to be happy and the only way I can fulfill my

The Culminate Amethyst

needs is to have multiple women, willingly, to satisfy my needs," he replied.

"Are you truly a prince?" she asked. "Were you dropped as a baby?"

"I am a prince and I will be king. We do not need to follow the rules your father has put in place for you," said Prince Domineer as he walked closer to her. "I can show you how strong I am," he began slowly. "You will love it and you will love me and you won't want anyone else but me." said the prince as she stopped him.

"No I will not. My heart is already taken for a suitor of my liking," she said as she watched him look disappointed and felt relieved.

"Well," began the prince with a smile. "He doesn't need to know about me and the nights that we would spend together. I can prove how good I am to you. You won't want him after you spend a night with me." said the prince as he continued to move closer to her. Then Aarilina stopped him with her hand. "Actually, I do mind and I like my nights uneventful."

"You like to be bored with uneventful nights?" asked the prince. "You poor girl."

"I like absolute silence," she said.

"How about a kiss, maybe that would change your mind," said the prince as he nudged his head forward to get a kiss from her.

"How about you kiss the door," she said, but the prince didn't respond and grabbed her arm as he dominated her. "I will not kiss you, now leave!" she continued and slapped the prince across the face and felt his tight grip on her arm.

"You will change your mind once I get my hands on the mask and you will serve me day and night," he said as he let go of her arm, opened the door, and left.

Princess Aarilinus took a deep breath and touched her arm. She thought about telling her father, but she knew he would not believe her. She closed the door and began to cry as she hoped Animus would find the mask before the selected princes did. It was only a matter of time before the mask would be found and she would be a prisoner in a marriage with the wrong man.

The day seemed to drag on for Animus and all he could do was dream of the princess. Every sunset reminded Animus of his beloved Aarilina and it was difficult for him to concentrate on his work.

Animus helped his father harvest the land since he was a boy. The peasant put his blood, sweat, and time into the chores. He remodeled the house and built the barn with his father as well as harvest the crops that were traded to people in Aria.

Animus daydreamed of kissing Aarilina and it rejuvenated his body from being exhausted from pitching hay. It would be days before the peasant would be able to visit Aarilina again. It was too dangerous to go back to the castle while there were visitors from others kingdoms.

Harvesting the land was a lot of work. Adam traded for food and money but it was difficult because nobles that favored the king as well as store and shop owners were choosing not to trade with Adam because they knew of his status with the king. They knew what he did in the past and didn't want to associate with him. The nobles and peasants that lived closer in the kingdom signed an agreement together to not do business with Adam. The king didn't know where Adam lived, but wanted Adam to lose everything and starve to death. Some of the people pitied Adam and secretly traded with him anyways.

Every night the Brokenheart family would spend time playing games; performing on musical instruments using carved wood and stretched skin for tom toms. The children performed as their own little musical band to entertain themselves.

The cottage was hidden in a forest on the border of Aria and they farmed a few acres of land that was owned by the original farmer who passed away and remained hidden under the farmer's name who was known as Clive Stump. They had some food that was grown, cotton from the farmland to make clothes with the use of a spinning wheel as well as wool from the herd of sheep to keep warm in the winter and domesticated animals to be butchered for meat. Adam and Olivia's fear was that one day the king would find them and take their lives.

There was limited room in the cottage and the four older siblings lived in the barn. Adam's wife and daughters produced all the clothes, blankets, quilts, and did all the cooking. Animus struggled for dominance against his brother Sydney who was a year younger than him. Even though they remained close they were completely different people. Aryan and Gabriel were into adventure and were more like their brother Animus. The two sisters Jada and Alexandria stayed to mend the house and watch over their baby brother Erike. Jada felt compelled to seek adventures like her brothers rather than follow in her mother's footsteps. Now at the age of sixteen she strayed away from being a lady to becoming a tomboy. Alexandria was the helpful guardian for Erike and remained invisible to other siblings because she didn't like conflict.

That evening, Animus sat down next to Adam as many times before. Through many troubles and hardships, the hospitality always worked out in the end of their hard work. Olivia who was the thinker conversed with Adam about uncertainty about the season they were in and spoke about Sydney's crime of stealing from the nobles.

"There is very little I can do to Sydney without throwing him out of the house," said Adam. "If we throw him out, we risk being discovered by the king."

"He needs to learn that if he continues to steal that there are consequences. We don't need him dragging the whole family into a big mess with the affairs of the king. He's a bad influence on our children."

"I'll have a talk with him," said Adam as he scratched his beard.

Adam was six foot four and a two-hundred fifty pound man with short black hair and a beard with a little bit of grey. He was in his forties and was trained by Clive on how to live off the land.

"Father, what do you know about the stories of the mask?" asked Animus as he took a bite from his carrots and potatoes. Adam turned to Animus as he was about to take a bite out of his potatoes and gravy. He remembered telling the stories to Animus as a child and took a bite of his food.

"You mean the legend of Furrengee?" asked Adam.

Just then, there was a break at the door that interrupted the conversation. The old door handle would always stick to the rest of the metal components and required a good kick to get it to open. It was Aryan and Gabriel and they had returned from setting raccoon traps. They closed the door behind them and took off their hats and coats.

"Where's Sydney?" asked Olivia.

"He decided to go into town to barter with the store owners," replied Gabriel.

"More like steal," added Adam as he turned his attention to Animus.

"Are you talking about the stories I told you to put you to sleep?" he continued.

"Yes, can you tell me more about the mask, does it exist?" asked Animus.

All was quiet and Animus was interested in getting answers than eating the rest of his foods. Erike and Alex talked among themselves of their oldest brother's ambitions.

"Animus is in love and just wants to get the mask to marry the princess," teased Alexandria with a big grin.

"You think you can mind your own business! If you're not going to eat go change the stalls in the barn," he replied as his face turned red from being embarrassed.

Animus closed his eyes and had second thoughts about Furrengee even being real. He realized the legend was probably nothing more than a fairy tale. He wondered through all the stories that father shared, was there anything relevant. Perhaps a story that he didn't hear that revealed some truth to Furrengee. All the answers about the mask that held unimaginable power was hidden in stories by Adam and only Adam. Very little was heard by angels in the kingdom. The elders told Animus what they knew, which was very little. The king removed all books and stories from the universities and those that talked about it were executed and killed.

"Son do you seek the mask for Princess Aarilinus?" asked Adam.

"Look, just forget it," replied Animus as his lips trembled while taking a spoonful of his peas into his mouth and looked away.

"It's silly you risk your heart for that girl, when the king strives to kill you," replied Adam in a stern voice as he crossed his arms while sitting in the chair and watched his son turn his head to look in Adam's eyes.

"The king sent a proposal and agreements to five princes' who seek Aarilina's hand in marriage for the retrieval of the mask."

"You believe the king will honor the agreement with you that are meant for the princes?" asked Adam cautiously as he watched Animus nod slowly. "I think we should have a talk."

Animus' father set the fork next to his plate and rose up from his chair as Animus stood up. They both walked outside and watched the stars shine.

"Beautiful night," said Adam as he let out a sigh, but suddenly heard a small nudge at the door and opened it to reveal eaves droppers. Alexandria and Erike were near the back of the door listening to what they were saying.

"Could you excuse us?" replied their father as he slowly pushed them away with his hands, gesturing them to leave.

"Let's go for a walk," said Adam changing his mind as he turned to his son and led Animus from the porch into the meadow of the front yard.

Animus felt a cool breeze run through his long blond hair, the night sky revealed more of the stars as the clouds could not be found in the sky. They walked across the yard to a wooden swing bench that was faced sideways with the house on the left and the crops to the right.

Animus remembered when he was little and played with his brothers and sisters. He could hear his sibling's voices arguing and pretending while they were sword fighting, which put a smile on his face.

After the flashback was gone and they both sat next to each other on the old swing bench. It seemed like yesterday that they were children and now they were all almost grown up. Adam stretched his arms and hands out as though he were reaching for the sky and yawned.

"Tell me about the mask, father?" asked Animus.

"The king wants to use the mask for his own purpose," replied Adam as he looked at his son and danced around the question before answering. "The mask grants its possessor the power of invincibility."

"So the stories are true," said Animus as he looked to the ground and then back at his father. "I need to get the mask."

"No you don't," said Adam.

"I need to do this for myself."

"Getting the mask will get you killed."

"Not if you help me."

"I don't know if I can help you," said Adam.

"How will I succeed?" asked Animus.

"Forget about her."

"Forget about who?" asked Animus.

"You know who I'm talking about, son. You've been very sneaky, going into the castle and I watched you run away from the house to play with her since you were seven years old," replied Adam with a serious look. "You're lucky you haven't been killed by her father."

"I can't forget her," replied Animus as he continued. "She's a part of me."

His father became silent and lowered his head to the ground. Animus took a deep breath and turned his head away knowing, deep in his soul, he was facing his destiny. Adam looked at his son and saw himself eighteen years ago. He knew there was no way to talk Animus out of pursuing Princess Aarilinus. He got up from the bench and walked around to stretch his legs and to think.

"Did the king give the suitors a map of the Furrengee Citadel?"

"I don't know. I didn't know there was a map of the citadel."

"He probably doesn't care because he wants the mask," said Adam. "How are you going to find your way around the temple without a map?"

"I don't know. I don't even know where the citadel is ," began Animus. "So I'll have to follow someone to the temple and when I get inside I'll have to try and stay alive."

"The citadel is a death trap. Anybody who enters will die from the creatures that are there," said Adam.

"There has got to be a way," said Animus as he looked at his father and got a long pause.

"There is a way," answered Adam with a smile.

Animus smiled and realized there was hope. With such courage Animus looked into his father eyes and listened to him talk about the mask.

"The mask is inside a temple within a mountain known as Shadow Mountain. Animus, in the wrong hands, the mask will destroy anybody that wishes to use it for evil. The mask can't be used to attack a human being. It can only be used to defend and kill anyone who isn't human."

"How do you know so much about the mask?" asked Animus. "Tell me, I need to know about the past."

"I was a young man," Adam began while walking a few steps away from Animus and turned around to look in his son.

"I was your age and heard stories of Shadow Mountain that had the mask. The old king and queen who ruled Aria were merciful and diplomatic until their early deaths. The young prince, Ruke Owen, married a young woman named, Aarilina and two years later they had a daughter. The queen died during child birth leaving King Owen alone with his daughter. My impression of the new king was that he was treacherous, greedy and spoiled and he still is. This makes him more dangerous."

The baby survived and was declared by prophets as the most beautiful child in the kingdom. Following the rumors of the princess was the legend of Furrengee. He was a mighty warrior, who inspired men to slay creatures that threatened the land. The stories of Furrengee became an epic that revealed Furrengee being caught in a deadly love triangle which got him killed. The legend says that his mask has secret powers and invincibility. Just before Ruke became king, darkness found its way into Aria from the death of Ruke's parents, the old king and queen. After he became king, the kingdom got worse and fell into despair. The good tree that bared its fruit was rotted.

King Owen chose to be wicked even while he was with his wife. After his queen died he only got worse and when he learned the mask could bring back Queen Aarilinus. He sent hundreds of knights and warriors into the Furrengee Citadel, which got them all killed. The mask was left unreachable and King Owen stopped sending his best knights to retrieve it," said Adam as he paused and then continued.

"Two years passed and everyone forgot about the mask and became concerned with the king and his daughter. Then there was a rogue warrior who got possession of the mask and used it to take back his lost love that was stolen from him. Everything in his path was crushed, warriors were set on fire and all was set aside to spend eternity with the beautiful handmaiden. Once the mask was renounced a knight stole it and put the mask on. The mask immediately vaporized the knight in the blink of an eye. King Owen took ownership of the mask, but never put it on to bring back his dead wife."

"Why not?" interrupted Animus as his eyebrows raised with curiosity.

"Well, because he was scared," said Adam. "You have to be a good person to wear the mask and King Owen isn't a good person."

"Then why does he want it if he is scared to wear it?" asked Animus.

"Well, probably because he doesn't want anyone else to wear it," said Adam as he continued.

"Text written by scribes and historians say the mask is haunted by evil spirits, legend says they're the fiduciaries of the mask. I stole the mask from the king and returned it to the citadel because I was finished using the mask and the king had no business keeping it for himself. The mask is powerful and has been worn by many great warriors."

"So you were the one who got the mask. Were you the one who the king hates so much?"

"Well there is more and it goes deeper than you think," said Adam

"Please go on," said Animus.

"I was in love with a woman who was the king's handmaiden, she was your mother. I endured everything to see her, until the king made it clear that anyone who wasn't a noble or a knight would not be allowed to lay eyes on his property. My love affair was discovered by the knights and we were taken to the king. It was the queen who convinced the king to spare our lives. I was exiled from Aria, but that didn't stop me. I kept seeing her and secretly married her before you were born. When the queen died and King Owen lost his mind. You were born in the castle and kept a secret from the king by handmaidens for a year until you both could be freed. Before I was able to get the mask, there was a suspicion by the king that the princess, who was just born, was going to be murdered."

"You were the rogue," began Animus with a smile. "My mother was the king's handmaiden? This sounds like a fairy tale."

"It's more than a fairy tale it's the secret of why we live the way we do and keep outside the kingdom."

"So what does this have to do with Aarilina?" repeated Animus.

"When I put the mask on to rescue your mother, I charged the castle gates and nothing could stop me, no fire, steel or wood could stand in my way. The king cursed at me that he would have my head and the mask. My anger indulged itself and was unleashed in a curse to the heir of the thrown. The fiduciaries agreed upon the curse and a lesson was to be learned that the love of his family was more important than the fate of the mask. The king knows I am responsible for the fate of his daughter. Son, I'm afraid fate will fall upon you and Princess Aarilinus will die. She will die from the blade of a broken heart and it will arrive on her seventeenth birthday, the age that her mother past away," Adam said sadly.

"That is why you and mom wanted me to abandon her," began Animus calmly.

"I didn't realize how much you were in love with her," began Adam. "I thought you would learn that she's royalty and belongs with a prince, but as it turns out your attachment is going to cost you emotionally."

"You lied to me, I look ahead of my life, thinking everything was great my head held high. Now you're telling me there is nothing I can do and I should forget about her," said Animus.

"You can do anything you want as long as you put your mind to it. If you proclaim the mask before she turns seventeen and keep her from marrying anyone who is not in love with her, only then will the curse be broken."

There was a steady silence between Animus and Adam as they tried to figure out how this catastrophe could be averted. Aarilina would have wanted him to see past this and fight for her.

"Three days?" whispered Animus.

"What?" asked Adam.

"Three days," he repeated.

"Three days."

"Aarilina's birthday is in three days."

"Then there is time, there is still hope to undo what once was wrong!" said Adam with confidence.

They walked back into the house and Animus followed his father to his parent's room. Adam opened up a hidden compartment in the floor and pulled out a large rolled up, yellow, piece of paper.

"I drew this map to get the mask while you were in the castle," began Adam with a pause. "Think very carefully, you will face things you could never imagine. Are you willing to risk your life for her?" asked Adam as he watched Animus hesitate.

"I would die for her."

It was dawn and in Aarilina's room were two handmaidens, Melody and Anastasia, who had just finished helping the princess get her dress on. It was big and beautiful and was one of her mother's dresses. It was worn before she was born and as she looked in the mirror and wondered what her mother was like. Aarilina didn't know if she was going to be meeting a lot of nobles and friends of father who would converse with her about her suitors. Or would she be conversing with soldiers or knights in case the day was uneventful. The handmaidens were around her, styling her hair and applying ointment and makeup. They were the same age and grew up with her since they were children.

"Have you met Prince Tusk? I hear he is unbelievable," said Anastasia.

"He's unbelievably disruptive," answered the princess in a cold tone.

"Have you heard of Prince Domineer? Word spreads that he is quite the legend in the bedroom?" said Melody.

"Oh yes, I hear he enchants women from great distances to make sweet, passionate, love to them," laughed Anastasia.

"I think he's disgusting," answered Princess Aarilinus.

Princess Aarilinus' hair was perfect and so was her face with the applications of makeup and lipstick. Aarilina was handed a mirror and saw herself as a work of art. The princess thought to herself; *all I need is Animus to rescue me from this nightmare.*

"You look beautiful your highness, don't you think?" asked Melody.

Princess Aarilinus smiled in the mirror, "yes I do."

She turned her head from the mirror to the top of her desk and grabbed her diary. She opened it to make sure the letter for Animus was there and then closed it. Melody saw the name Animus on the envelope and knew who he was.

"Do you miss Animus?" asked Melody.

"Imagine a man who could make you feel so happy that you would want nothing more," she replied.

Both handmaidens became quiet as they stepped aside for the princess to get up from her stool. Princess Aarilinus rose up and looked around for a place to hide her diary. She walked over to her dresser and hid the diary between the dresser drawers.

"You will keep our conversation a secret from my father is that understood," she commanded.

"Yes your majesty," said Melody.

"We won't tell anyone you love Animus," said Anastasia.

"Thank you."

Now the princess could continue the day and walk with her bodyguard around the castle grounds. With one foot stepped outside of her bedroom, she began walking down the stairs with her trusted handmaidens behind her until they ran into Jenna.

"My lady, you have got to meet Prince Corsair from Sporsindor. He has come to meet with you," chuckled Jenna.

"No more visits," answered the princess.

"My lady, he is a handsome gentleman and wants to meet you. You're all dressed up so nice with your beautiful dress, go speak to him," encouraged Jenna.

"I'll speak to him if it makes you happy," sighed the princess with a feeling that he would be another Prince Tusk or worse Prince Domineer.

"Girls, I need you to tend to the gardens," ordered Jenna to Melody and Anastasia.

Aarilina followed Jenna to the library where people bowed as she passed. Tables were filled with peasants, squires, pages and handmaidens reading stories and text books of many different subjects. She was led by Jenna to a table where a man with shoulder length, sandy blond, hair and green eyes looked at her while he remained sitting. He was dressed in silk clothes and had a small freckle on his upper right cheek.

"Your highness, allow me to introduce myself, my name is Prince Corsair," he smiled.

Aarilina looked at Jenna as her eyebrows raised with excitement and smiled, "I'll leave you two alone."

All was quiet, and Aarilina tried to decide where to begin with her conversation. Things seemed fuzzy in the Princess' mind; her stomach felt tight and queasy as though someone had just jumped up and down on her diaphragm like a trampoline.

"I'm happy to meet you and I would like to spend part of the day as your guest," said Corsair.

"Very well, I can do that," she answered with a tone as though was was walking on egg shells. Since her last two visits with the two princes' were disappointing she didn't have a high opinion on any of the suitors.

Prince Corsair led the way out of the library and outside the garden where handmaidens as well as other servants were busy planting baby trees. Aarilina felt as though he was known from another life. He was kind like Animus and spoke only when there was something nice to say.

"How do you feel about becoming queen?" he asked with a smile.

"To tell you the truth, I don't feel anything for it but my people need me," she replied.

"But think about the positive changes you could bring to your people," he said.

Aarilina grinned with a raised eyebrow and thought to herself; there was a lot of good in being a queen. She looked at Prince Corsair and wanted to believe he was a good man, but didn't want to believe everything he said. The princess never did explain in detail what would be done to bring peace and love.

"There are positive changes I would make for Aria," began the princess.

"Really? Would you care to share?" he asked.

"Later," said the princess as she hesitated before continuing. "What kind of king would you be?"

"All right," began Corsair slowly as he stopped and looked into her eyes.

"I'm a good king, just and fair. In my kingdom, we would have balls everynight, full training for the knights, archery, fencing and boxing," answered Corsair.

"So how would you keep your people happy?" asked Aarilina.

"Archery, fencing, boxing and other contests and training to be a knight," he repeated.

"What if they don't want to be a part of any of that?" she asked.

"What would you do?" he asked.

"It's not what I would do, but what kind of a king would let his queen do the things she needs to do," answered Aarilina with a smile as she watched Corsair smile back.

"Is that a question? Forgive me your highness my idea of greatness was not just for me alone, but for you and my people," answered the prince as he touched her wrist gently.

Aarilina closed her eyes and nodded as she felt like Animus was in front of her because of how closely he resembled him. *Was it bad for a man to feel powerful from the strength of his queen?* She thought to herself. No, but it was questionable if she would hear her own voice call upon the power of her people to defend their way of life from enemies.

There was a part of Corsair that was sweet and innocent like Animus, but Corsair was a prince and had great honor. The funny thing about meeting Prince Corsair was she began thinking more about Animus.

"I wrote a song for you," continued Corsair as Aarilinus' removed her hand from his and then he knew there was something wrong.

"Is there someone else in your life?" he asked to confirm his intuition.

"Does it matter?" she asked.

"It matters to me," said Corsair.

"I've known him for a long time."

"Would I be able to win your heart by beating him in this contest for the mask?"

"No," she answered firmly.

The Culminate Amethyst

"What does this man have that I don't?"

"Lord Corsair, I don't want to talk about this. Inviting you here was my father's idea," she answered as she turned her back to the prince and walk away.

Oh darling you look nice
your eyes are warm like the sun
your voice is beautiful like the chirping of robins
when you walk past the trees and shrubs
you bring them into bloom

Princess Aarilina stopped and turned around as she looked into his eyes after a few feet of walking. She didn't expect a prince to suddenly start singing and he had a good voice that relaxed her. She blushed and felt a little embarrassed, but the feeling subsided and she smiled.

"Not bad, but your composition isn't creative because your words don't rhyme," she said with a smile and heard the prince sulk at her.

"Poems don't have to rhyme! You didn't give me a chance to finish," he complained.

"I apologize, my lord, please continue," she answered.

oh darling you look nice
your eyes are warm like the sun
your voice is beautiful like the chirping of robins
when you walk past the trees and shrubs
you bring them into bloom

oh Aarilina I can't escape your voice
it's like the fire streaming from the sun
oh Aarilinus I don't know how to make a choice
all I want to do is fulfill the mystery of fun
until the sunsets upon the world and the moon shines on us.

Aarilina smiled because the poem was sweet. For once she met a prince that wasn't deranged. His eyes melted into hers and she knew he had a good heart.

"I'll see you at the masquerade in two days," said Prince Corsair as he bowed his head and left.

"A masquerade, what is father planning?" she whispered to herself as her bodyguard walked up behind her. Together they left the library and went outside to begin their walk around the castle grounds to get some light exercise.

A day without Animus was long and difficult for the princess. She could feel goosebumps cover her legs from the cold breeze of the cloudy summer morning. It was nice to walk the trails outside the castle without father worrying about her. With permission from the king, she was able to walk with her bodyguard on the trails. Her father freaked out if she was outside the castle grounds with no protection, which made her feel like a prisoner.

It was the afternoon and the clouds unveiled the sun and the light hit the princess as she felt the heat hit her body. She was no longer cold, but now she was getting hot. Her eyes squinted from the blindness of the sun to see the long path ahead and sweat began to perspire on her forehead. She opened up her white, fancy, umbrella so she wouldn't burn in the sun. They came across a park area with a bench and they decided to stop to take a break.

"Thank you," said the princess as the bodyguard laid down a blanket and helped her sit on the bench.

The hours of walking were harsh for the princess to and she grew tired of being followed by the servant. When she was ready to get up, she looked at her bodyguard who looked like he was waiting for a catastrophe. She got back up and continued walking. The body guard followed her and she noticed he held the handle of his sword. The walk next to the trees gave them some shade momentarily until they walked back into the sun again. She could tell this soldier was stressed and acted like a gang of ogres were going to charge and run off with her. She felt nothing, but over protection and only the loud clang sound of his metal armor could be heard.

She turned to look at her bodyguard and asked, "are you stressed?"

"No your highness."

"Then why won't you talk to me?"

"I was ordered not to. No small talk," he replied.

"What is your name?" she asked, but didn't get an answer and stopped walking.

"Tell me your name bodyguard," she ordered

"Sir Edward Bobbit," he answered.

Then the princess remembered him and knew he was one of the lowest ranking soldiers. Edward Bobbit was a young, twenty year old, man with no family or friends. He was about five-foot nine and one-hundred and thirty pounds with an average build. In a way Aarilina felt sorry for him and wanted him to loosen up.

"We've walked around the second gate for hours and you've said nothing of my dress today. Is it pretty or does it surfeit you?" she asked.

"Your beauty has been heard and seen throughout the kingdom. I know how beautiful you are, but the king has spies watching us and if he finds out what is taking place I'll be punished."

"My father threatens you for a harmless question?" she asked

"Yes your highness."

"Are you hot wearing your armor?"

"Yes your highness."

"Then take it off," she replied, but got a peculiar expression from his eyes.

"Fear not, I will protect you against my father. Look upon me as you would no other and answer my question," she insisted with a smile.

The bodyguard thought for a minute and realized she was right. After all, she was going to be his future queen. Edward Bobbit took off his armor and after kneeling down to take the final piece of metal from his ankle he looked at the princess. He was taller than her with short black hair and brown eyes. He knew the princess was beautiful but now he was able to soak her figure in his eyes and realized she was much more than he thought.

"Hello, are you going to tell me?" she asked and started laughing.

The servant kneeled himself to the ground and started crying. The princess gently put her hand on his head and pitied him for being miss-treated by her father.

"You are the most beautiful woman I have ever seen," he replied as he sat on the grass bare footed.

"Have you not seen a woman before, one that holds such beauty and grace?" she asked with a smile and continued. "Sir Edward Bobbit have you even seen a beautiful woman before?" she asked but got no reply. "It's ok, our secret is safe. All I want you to do is answer my question, do you not like my dress today?"

"You look lovely your highness," he answered.

"Thank you. You see, that wasn't so hard," she said.

"No it wasn't," he said as he got up from the ground with a smile and continued their walk. Sir Edward Bobbit left his armor hidden behind some bushes behind a tree.

"It's such a beautiful day! I like the way the clouds curl themselves into each other," she said with a smile realizing she was now having a lot of fun with her bodyguard instead of the boring status of how he was before.

"It is and it complements you. Without you we would have no beautiful days," said Edward. "You're the essence of beauty."

"Thank you Edward and thanks for making this day memorable for me," she said. "Edward, I want you to play a game with me."

"A game?" he asked with a strange look.

"It's very simple, you lie down facing the ground and count until you can count no further and then you try to find me."

"I don't believe that is so, my lady, my job is to protect you. Not play games with you."

"Yes, except father wishes for my happiness. A princess can only take so much protection before she goes absolutely insane."

"I see," began Edward as he ran his fingers through his black hair and thought about it.

"Ok," he replied puzzled with a sigh as he lied down on the grass and started counting.

Princess Aarilinus ran far to the township area, to an area hidden from the people, in a forest, and hidden in an old, condemned, church that was transformed into what she called The Clandestine Garden. It was a building that was overgrown with trees, flowers and a deep pool in the center. Nobody knew about it because it was hidden and the water was always clear. The water was nice and warm and the animals came for sanctuary.

"I thought I would never lose him," she whispered to herself as she stretched her arms and hands outward and she raised her head up to the broken chandelier to embrace the warmth of the sun that shined from above.

There were many visits to this special place by Aarilina before the trees, plants and flowers filled the building with beauty. Erosion gave her the inspiration to create the pool with Animus, when they were children, and now there was something special to remember.

The princess took off her shoes and socks to dip her toe in the water. She felt the warm water and confirmed the water was nice. Aarilina set her shoes, her crown on the ground and unraveled her hair from its braids. She walked to the edge of the pool and realized she didn't want to get the dress, her mother wore, soiled but she didn't have anything else to wear and realized it was worth the risk.

The princess looked around and realized she was alone in the garden as well as her life without Animus. She knew she wasn't innocent and took off the dress to swim in the water. Aarilina felt like she was living in a cage with the expectations of her father to fulfill an illusions to make him happy. To make him glorified, honorable and powerful.

She splashed the water with her hands, feet and slowly removed her worries of rules and expectations as she became one with the water. With each movement of her hands and feet to the deeper part of the pool. She felt she was in uncharted waters in her life and a frog, that was large, swam up to the lilly pad and climbed onto it. The lilly pads joined her from the edge of the pool and the princess could see that the water lillies had bloomed. She hymned and rose from the water to sit on the ledge and felt the cold stone texture with her naked body. The princess' long, black, hair stuck to her back as she moved to sit under the sun and felt the heat on her face and it made her feel good. She continued to hymn and sing the song that she wrote for Animus.

I circle around in the night sky
waiting for you to arrive to me
I got desire that burns in my heart
it is what you want, it is what I need
with the impressions I must heed

like magic it is
like magic it is
like magic it is

I circle around the beautiful night sky
I'm down to say this, sad good-bye
if I can't have you I would rather die
but I know that you are coming
yes I do, deep in my heart
from me to you
because it's almost like magic

like magic it is
like magic it is
like magic it is

Princess Aarilinus' eyes blinked as she saw the butterflies fly to her and kiss her head. She started laughing because they tickled her face and then after they left, one of the butterflies landed on her palm. She giggled as a few more landed and tickled the palm of her hand.

There was a sound of something moving in the brush and she looked to see a fox peek at her from behind a tree. It didn't come across as threatening and looked at her curiously.

"Come here," she said with a smile and gestured with her hand.

Aarilina cracked a grin as she rose up from the ledge and walked towards it. The fox sat down by the tree and waited for her. She heard the birds chirping for her to continue the hymn, but she wanted to meet her new friend, the fox.

She knew her voice enchanted the fox and other animals with her singing. The princess knew they admired her and wanted to be with her because she was different than any human they knew of.

Aarilina walked over to the fox and stopped a foot away and leaned her hand out. The fox smelled her hand and then moved up against her chest to lick her face. She smiled while looking around and watched the roses and tulips move from the wind as it blew her hair. Two robins glided down from a tree and land on her shoulders. They chirped as she pet the fox's head and giggled.

The king stepped inside his daughter's room and was looking for her diary. He knew she had one because he watched her write in it outside. It was a book with all of her secrets and thoughts of what was going on in her life.

He kneeled beside the bed and reached within the silk bedspread as well as under the fabric of the mattress. A deep sigh breached his breath and he suddenly looked at the dresser. King Owen walked to his daughter's dresser, ran his fingers upon its smooth wooden texture and remembered that it belonged to his wife.

The king kneeled down and stretched his arms under the dresser to feel for the diary. His fat fingers returned empty handed and his patience was wearing thin. King Owen gripped each of the dresser draws and pulled them out.

Suddenly, he heard something fall on the floor and looked at the book made of green leaves combined with little red and blue flowers, it was the diary.

King Owen flipped through each page after reading and his eyebrows protruded in anger to every word of love written for Animus. Animus was viewed as the prince and her father was portrayed as the idiot with power. There were so many mean words written by his daughter about him that it was like having his insides ripped out.

All of a sudden, a folded piece of paper slipped out and after King Owen dried his eyes with his hand. He picked up the piece of paper and expected it to be another diary entry that was going to be discarded. His eyes widened with anger to learn she was planning to meet Animus tomorrow night at Humming Forest. The king folded the letter and placed it back in the diary.

Minutes seemed like hours, King Owen sat on her bed and was trying to decide what to do next. He fought countless battles against enemies and made himself a legend throughout the land as the protector of Aria, but for the first time in his life he stood next to himself struggling with how to fix the relationship with his daughter that was dead. She would believe him and thank him when he was done with her.

King Owen slid the diary back under the dresser drawer and picked up the mess left on the floor. Then he realized he was left with his original goal which was to get rid of Animus, permanently, and force her to believe he was right.

A big gold fish jumped up a foot from the water and back down into the water. The princess was underwater and looked up from the bottom of the pool. She pushed with her feet to the surface to take a breath.

When she reached the surface, she gasped for air and splashed water everywhere. She went back underwater and continued to swim with joy. The garden seemed magical, but there was nothing magical about it. The Clandestine Garden was a place for her when she wanted to be left alone and forget who she was alone, but the animals didn't see it that way. They saw it as a place to go, a haven, to keep them safe from the hostile world.

Princess Aarilinus felt warmth from the sun as she remained in the water and thought about Animus. The feeling of being in love with Animus sent shivers throughout her body as she took a deep breath and went underwater. Aarilina swam underwater and remembered when she played with Animus as a little girl. It was quiet and peaceful underwater and when she heard Animus' voice as a boy, she smiled; *do you think we'll be friends forever?* Then of course she remembered what she told him; *of course we'll be friends forever, you silly boy.* Aarilina remembered all the adventures while they were together and could see the light from the sun go through the water. It was beautiful and was like flying in one of her dreams.

Seconds turned to minutes and the inside of her chest began to hurt. She pushed her feet from the bottom of the pool and resurfaced to take a deep breath of fresh air. Aarilina took a couple deep breaths and swam to the ledge where she saw the fox look at her. She raised herself up to the edge of the pool and saw that there were more animals looking at her from behind the trees. She ignored them and concentrated on what she was going to do next.

The princess forgot that her bodyguard was looking for her from the game, hide and seek, they were playing and realized she would have a lot of explaining to do. She pulled her wet hair back with her hand and stood up. It was time to leave and she thought about her letter to Animus, where they would embrace each other in an hour like no other. Then the princess saw the fox run away, as well as the other animals and the garden became empty.

Suddenly, there was a loud gasp, "what in Ayana are you doing child!" Princess Aarilinus turned her head in shock to see who it was and replied, "swimming naked."

"Are you crazy? Do you know how fast rumors would spread throughout the kingdom of this display?" asked Jenna as she quickly unraveled a towel that she carried for herself on the way home and covered the princess' body.

"How did you find me?"

The dark haired woman, with grey strands in her hair, looked at the princess puzzled. She remembered how much work it was to raise when she was a little girl. The princess was always running around, getting into trouble and knew that she was headed in the wrong direction from being a lady.

"What difference does it make? I was passing by and heard you singing," replied Jenna as she dried Aarilina's face and hair. In the princess' mind the handmaiden was old, worn and boring, but loyal to the family. Aarilina felt the maiden was a square and broke no rules to have fun. In many ways Jenna reminded Aarilina of her father and wondered, sometimes, who's side she was on.

"Princess you can't be doing this," began Jenna. "Soon you will be heir to the throne and setting an example to all girls of the virtue you have! Do you understand?" demanded Jenna as she leaned down to dry Aarilina's legs.

"No I don't, why don't you explain it to me?" asked the princess with a coy tone in her voice.

She could not keep herself from grinning and covered her mouth to keep Jenna from seeing her smile. Aarilina was tired of being babysat by father's soldiers, maidens, guards and other dubious figures that it made sense to put on an act to be coy. It was fun and hilarious to watch people get angry, but hide their emotions around her because she was a princess.

"You're special Aarilina," began Jenna as she looked into her eyes. "You will inspire the nation of Aria of what it means to love, honor and protect those that are innocent and nothing negative must be sought against you because mothers of those daughters depend on you. They depend on your image for their daughters to aspire."

"Please Jenna, spare me the talk. I'm an ordinary girl who wants to experience life."

"You break my heart child and your mother's," replied Jenna. "Everybody has this image of their future queen that she is the star that shines pure goodness and if anyone should see you like I found you today it would destroy that image of the perfect person you will soon be."

"Nobody saw me, I assure you," replied the princess as she watched the handmaiden hesitate.

"Now, the first thing we have got to do is put some clothes on you," declared the handmaiden as she grimaced and found the princess' dress hanging on the tree on the other side of the pool. After reclaiming it, Jenna helped Aarilina get dressed.

"Did you know my mother?" she asked.

"I knew your mother well, she was beautiful, kind, honorable lady and was like a sister to me. She dreamed of excitement, but never got to pursue it. I see her everyday as I watch you grow," smiled Jenna.

Aarilina looked at Jenna with kindness and wiped her eyes, "I wish I knew my mother."

"She was a wonderful woman and a great queen," said Jenna as she zipped up the back of her dress. "Now, would you tell me what you were really doing?" repeated Jenna.

"I wanted to be alone, I was daydreaming of my lover. We use to go swimming together," Aarilina smiled.

"With your clothes on, I hope," said Jenna.

"Yes, today was an exception because I didn't want to ruin my dress," said Aarilina as she closed her eyes and smiled.

"Oh, your birthday is coming up in two days how do you feel about being seventeen?" asked Jenna.

"I don't know, it feels as plain as any other number I've reached and I feel I'll be a sad queen for Aria. Father feels I should marry someone who better deserves me, but I'm in love with a peasant. His name is Animus and I feel he is right for me. Have you ever been in love?" asked the princess as she looked at Jenna.

"I imagine I have one time or another, but then I realized my place is here at the castle to serve the king. This Animus is the one you truly love?"

"Yes," replied Princess Aarilinus.

"Why? He's a peasant," said Jenna. "Prince Corsair is a prince and has much to offer ."

"Why does it matter what title of nobility my love holds as long as he loves me?" asked Aarilina. "Prince Corsair couldn't possibly love me in the future, he doesn't even know me. Animus and I have had a history together since childhood, we belong together."

Aarilina could tell she struck a nerve with Jenna by the expression on her face and by the way she spoke, "now, the first thing we have to do is to get you to your room and ready for the royal feed before your father erupts."

The princess and handmaiden walked out of the secret hiding place to find Edward Bobbit still looking for her by the castle and had his armor back on. They walked back to the castle together and got ready for the social hour. Edward Bobbit was relieved to see the princess again and joined them in their walk back to the Mid Tower.

It was drawing near for the royal feed and all the knights were prepared to rejoice with Princess Aarilinus. Prince Tusk and Prince Domineer were not invited to come because King Owen wanted to spend the time with his knights and daughter.

Sir Edward Bobbit sat in his chair in the throne room with the long broad table, with twenty of the knights. Sir Edward Bobbit tried to keep his mind clear, but couldn't. He was scared that he was going to be punished for losing the princess.

At last, Princess Aarilinus entered the dinning room in a beautiful, silk, emerald colored dress with Jenna and took her seat next to her father. Her hair was up in a braid and she looked exquisite with her makeup. Some of the knights had known the princess since she was born and watched her mature slowly into the young woman before them. King Owen rose his wine to prepare a toast as he looked at Sir Edward Bobbit and turned to his daughter with a smile, but looked like he was hiding something.

"Father," she said wondering what he was thinking.

"Long live, my daughter as queen," declared the king as servants walked by the table with plates of food for everyone to feast.

A plate of delicious looking food was set in front of Aarilina. It was her favorite dish of broccoli with cheese melted on top and roast beef. Her lips plucked outward with a smile as she spiked a broccoli from her plate and noticed the king was looking at her as she ate slowly. She felt him looking at her and wondered what was wrong. Her birthday was coming up and he was in a rush to get her in love with a prince and live happily ever after.

"For the future of Aria," declared the king while raising his goblet as everyone cheered and took a sip from their wine. The princess took a sip of her wine and laughed with everyone as they conversed. Aarilina smiled and laughed again at the knights who joked about their lives and realized these men were her family.

"So what plans does the princess have when she becomes queen?" asked Sir Anson.

"She is going to do the life long commitment that I've been waiting for since she was born," replied King Owen. "She's going to lead our kingdom and make it strong."

"Are we preparing to join the neighboring kingdoms for peace?" asked the middle aged knight, Sir Seres. "I heard three of the princes are here and we're still waiting for the other two."

"I wrote five letters to the kingdoms of Kalindor, Sporsindor, Endswood, Aryan and Stalous for a peace treaty," said King Owen. "We as a country need to stop and make peace with these kingdoms instead of making them our enemies."

"Has the princess chosen anyone to rule with?" asked Sir Norcom curiously.

"No, but we decided that the challenge will be the retrieval of the mask of Furrengee. The man who returns with the mask will win my daughter's hand," he declared.

Aarilina was thinking about Animus and remembered when they were thirteen years old, building Clandestine Garden and it started raining. She smiled as she remembered the drops of rain hitting her face.

"Animus come on, its raining we have to stop!" yelled Aarilina as the rain pelted her purple dress.

"We're not done yet, help me move this tree," he ordered as he picked up the small oak tree with his hands with its roots intact.

Aarilina helped him move it into a hole that they dug together. The tree was in the three foot hole and Aarilina held it in place as he buried the roots with the shovel. They were both dirty and Aarilina had mud on her face from planting flowers before it rained.

When Animus was finished he looked at her with a smile and she shook her head. He was a stubborn kid that wouldn't let nature dictate his life.

"You just don't give up do you," she said.

"I'm almost done Aarilina, I built this kingdom, this paradise out of

nothing and I did it for you."

Aarilina smiled and couldn't help it, she ran up and kiss him. When they were finished they looked at each other and smiled.

"My father can destroy this place, but he can never destroy how I feel about you," she said.

Aarilina smiled as she remembered everything and realized they were still together, except now the stakes were much higher.

"Can we trust Prince Tusk?" asked Sir Norcom. "His father has tried to take over our kingdom many times before."

"Yeah, but that was years ago," said King Owen. "I spoke to his father and he wants to leave the feuds in the past and concentrate on the future."

"Yes, but a man who wounds a bear for attacking him doesn't look for the bear to sleep with him," said Sir Seres as he heard a burst of laughter from Anson and the other knights.

Princess Aarilinus laughed as well because the knight had a good point. She knew that father wanted these peace talks to go through, but the knights were wise and learned from the past that their enemies were envious of Aria, for its ability to defend its borders and innovation to attract wealth.

"Sir Bobbit, did I not give you orders to watch my daughter?" asked the king in a rough tone and in a cold stare.

Then the princess felt the shift in energy from the other knights. Everyone knew King Owen had a big temper and Aarilina felt her arms become numb.

"Yes your highness, but she ordered me to engaged in a game so she wouldn't be bored sir," stuttered Edward Bobbit in fear.

"Ah I see," began King Owen as he looked around at the other knights. "I give rules for my knights to follow not to break whenever it suits them. Sir Jenkins when I give out my orders do I not expect them to be carried out?"

"Yes your majesty," replied Sir Jenkins with an unpleasant look of regret.

"Father it was I who disobeyed your order, be merciful and spare Sir Bobbit," said the princess.

King Owen turned his head to his daughter after thinking about what to do next. He rubbed his hand against his bristly face as he tried to think of an adequate punishment.

"I was unsatisfied and needed some entertainment! Sir Edward Bobbit would not tell me if he liked my dress until I ordered him," continued Aarilina.

King Owen was silent with a disdain look in his eyes, "what? He looked at you."

"Well yes father, I am a woman who desires the attention of her faithful subjects."

"Do you take me for a fool? What kind of behavior is this?" asked the king.

"You mistreat me in front of the knights and show me off to the princes like a prize when I'm your daughter. I'm not your toy or a colt and I'm not a piece of meat!" she declared and got a cold stare from her father.

"You're out of line," replied her father and Aarilinus felt herself sink in her chair.

"Torque Edward Bobbit's eyes from out of his sockets and exile him from Aria. No wait, there is a better way! The Dark Wolves will have supper early this evening. Guards, take Mr. Bobbit to the Dark Wolves!"

"What? No father you can't do this!" screamed Princess Aarilinus.

"Someday you'll understand why I'm king. I can't allow our bodyguard to share to others what he has allowed to happen. It will ruin your future as queen," replied the king.

"I won't tell anyone, please, I beg you!" cried the bodyguard as he remained restraint under the guards and then taken away. Aarilina began to cry, she felt responsible and buried her face into her hands while crying.

Moments later, servants arrived with golden platters of strawberry crapes, fudge, cakes, frosted cup cakes and grapes. The king feasted his eyes on the food, except some of the knights who weren't happy with the decision the king made did not eat anything.

"Would you like to eat my dear?" asked King Owen and watched her raise her head to look at him.

"I lost my appetite?" she suspired and got up from the table to leave.

"Where are you going?" he demanded.

"There's something wrong with you, it was my fault and you're going to kill him. You didn't have to kill him!" she cried.

"Well then, next time you'll learn to follow my rules. Now tell me where are you going!" repeated the king.

"I'm going to my room!" yelled the princess.

"Maybe next time you'll think twice before you go swimming naked and make me a fool," said the king.

Aarilina stopped after she got up from her chair and looked at the king with her mouth dropped, "what? How dare you invade my privacy and set an example when I wanted to explore myself in privacy!"

King Owen said nothing and watched her look at Jenna who looked at Aarilina with guilt. The princess was angry and felt betrayed.

"I'm sorry, my child, it's my duty to tell the king everything," said Jenna.

"I thought I could trust you, my mother trusted you. You betrayed us both with what you shared today!" exclaimed Aarilina as she walked past the handmaiden and slammed the door and marched to her room.

The knights were quiet and some of them hardly ate, but King Owen continued to eat. There was no talking or laughing in the throne room, only the sound of the king filling his face with sweeties.

"Your majesty, don't you think you've been a little hard on your daughter ?" asked Sir Seres.

"Don't tell me how to raise my daughter," ordered the king.

"Yes, but your honor, she's the future queen," said Anson.

"Enough! She's turning seventeen and we've got to push this marriage through or else it's over!" yelled King Owen.

"What are you talking about?" asked Sir Jenkins.

Then the king became quiet and looked away from his knights, "never mind."

"Your majesty, I don't like this peace treaty with the other kingdoms," replied Sir Norcom.

"It's going to ensure the survival of Aria," began King Owen. "Aarilina needs a strong king to rule with her. I'm not going to live forever and you've always supported me before."

"I'm sorry your majesty," said Sir Jenkins looking confuse. "Something isn't right with this peace treaty."

Princess Aarilinus walked up the spiraling staircase thinking of the way father acted. A mind couldn't be more cluttered than a ball of yarn and she felt like she was dipped in honey and thrown onto a pile of hay.

With the turn of the door knob she felt at ease. She closed the door behind her and locked it before walking to the dresser and pulled out her diary. She relaxed on the bed and opened her diary to smell flowers from the pages. It was nice and sweet, but suddenly became quite discouraging when the letter she wrote was in the back of the book instead of the front where it was suppose to be. Aarilina's eyebrows protruded as she became angry and held the folded piece of paper in her right hand, realizing somebody was snooping around her room.

"I agree with the peace talks," said Jenna. "The princess needs a prince in her life, someone who's going to protect her, instead of this Animus."

"Yeah, you see!" yelled King Owen. "My handmaiden, who has been with me since my queen passed away, agrees that Aarilina needs someone better than a stupid peasant."

The knights were silent and looked at their king solemnly, expressing their need to defend Aria from any and all foreign powers. King Owen sat back in his chair with the feeling of being alone on this decision and knew he was on a slippery slope.

"Oh come on! I know what I'm doing, stand with me. Peace is at hand and so is the future of Aria. Lets drink to it," King Owen motioned and got the knight's mood to change.

The knights rejoiced and became drunk. They sang songs and ate fine food until the hour grew late. King Owen stopped Norcom from leaving the table.

"Yes your highness," said the knight who was the only one sober.

"Keep an eye on my daughter and let me know when she acts up," whispered the king sluggishly. "She's doing great folly against me and Aria with Animus and so you must help me stop her."

"As you wish," replied Sir Norcom with a nod.

The next morning arrived and Aarilina opened her eyes. She got out of bed and changed into her clothes. With great haste she ran downstairs to talk to the postman outside, to deliver her mail in secret.

"It's an urgent matter that is of great importance," ordered the princess.

"Yes your majesty," replied the postman as he took the envelope from her and looked at the address. "The address indicates it's outside the kingdom."

"Just follow the path that's hidden past the large oak tree. It turns into a road that leads to a house," said Aarilina.

"Yes your highness," said the man as he bowed his head and left.

Aarilina watched the postman get on his horse and leave through the castle gate. She hoped he would get to Animus in time so they could run away together.

The postman trotted on his horse to the first gate when suddenly a figure with a bow and arrow blocked his path. He was dressed in black armor with only his face revealed. He had brown eyes and hair with a little bit of white on his bangs.

"Can I help you sir?" asked the postman.

"Yes, you're delivering a letter for the princess and I wish to deliver it," said the man.

"I'm sorry, but under the authority of Aria I'm under no obligation to share mail with anyone, especially some thug off the street," replied the postman.

Suddenly, the man raised his bow and arrow, "give me the letter, I'm not going to ask again."

The postman looked around and saw five more men emerge from behind him and next to the bowman. The postman looked at the leader scared as he approached him.

Aarilina played many games of hide and seek with the children of the noble families. There was a dozen children that were left to be babysat to a couple handmaidens that volunteered to watch them for the day. The nobles had important business meetings with the king that involved tending their lands. There was an agreement that the nobles and the king made to keep the economy strong.

It was mid-afternoon and Princess Aarilinus laid down on the grass to watch the clouds veil the sun. There was little to do and the children were picked up by their parents to go home. The princess thought of the day she would have children with Animus, but then realized that it wouldn't happen because of father. He hated Animus and wanted him to disappear.

After visiting the library in the evening, the princess began having an unsettling feeling that she was being watched. As she walked down the hallway she could see the eyes of the paintings move which sent shivers throughout her body and she knew something was wrong.

Princess Aarilinus hid her fears and pretended everything was ok, but the eyes in the paintings, along the walls, watched her every move. She watched the painting's eyes move through the corner of her left eye and trembled. She felt goose bumps on her shoulders and began walking faster as she turned her eyes to see something run past behind her in the distance of the corridor. Aarilina turned around, only to find nothing was there. Her face started perspiring and her lips trembled while she took deep breaths and felt her heart beat faster. The princess lost control and ran with the two library books in each hand to make an abrupt turn to the next hallway and screamed.

The princess' outburst came as a surprise to the group of marching knights in the hallway. Her eyes and mouth remained wide open as her trembling body suddenly relaxed. She never felt this much anxiety other than the nightmares as a child.

"Are you ok, your highness," asked Sir Norcom as he walked over to her slowly.

Aarilina wiped the sweat from her forehead as she calmed down, "yes, I'm fine you just startled me."

Sir Norcom was quiet and looked at her with a serious look. It seemed clear that something was wrong and scared her. She would have to think of something else to encourage them that she would be fine.

"Do you want us to walk you to your room?" asked Sir Norcom

"No that's ok," she replied with a smile.

"We insist that we must protect our princess, even if it may be nothing," replied Sir Voles.

"Well thank you, I was headed to my room to sleep," she grinned as Sir Norcom held her hand and led her to her room. They walked into her room and he bowed his head to her.

"Well your highness, I'll leave you so you can get some rest."

"Thank you my knight, if I need anything I'll send for you," she said and watched him leave.

Aarilina yawned and lie down on her bed to get some sleep. Today was a busy day and the children exhausted her.

Princess Aarilinus opened her eyes after hearing the sounds of women and children crying and men yelling outside the window. She got out of bed and walked to the window only to find it had iron bars on it.

The princess clasped the bars as she started crying to what was witnessed. The feeling of being trapped in a room consumed her with destruction. She looked up at the full moon and to the fires lit upon the land, the gates were forged open and people were fighting in what looked like a war.

The setting of the sun split the sky into shades of red that looked like blood smeared on a canvas and the smell of death was in the air. Princess Aarilinus heard a sound and turned around to see father standing in front of her. It was the king, only he was burned and his clothes were tattered as though he had ran through a burning house.

"Father what happened to you?" cried Aarilina as the tears ran down her cheeks.

"You did this to me! You fell in love with that peasant and it cost me my kingdom!"

"Father please, don't," she begged as her lips trembled while seeing him raise a dagger. The princess' heart began beating hard as tears continued to fall from her eyes while her lips trembled.

"Now you're going to die!" the king bellowed as she looked at him in despair. Before the king could strike, a giant hand smashed through the barred window and gently took her. The princess was scared, but was happy to be safe from her father.

After all was well, the hand opened up and she was revealed to a giant wearing a mask. She looked up at the giant from the ground in a remote location as he suddenly shrank to the same size as her. He looked at her with his long beautiful, black, hair that was on the black, armor.

"Who are you?" she ordered.

"Furrengee," answered with a low deep voice behind the mask and the name echoed through her mind.

Aarilina woke up with a gasp, she never had a dream like that before and realized it was so real. Was it a message from the Burning Bush or Furrengee himself? She thought to herself. The princess hoped Animus got her letter and wanted to share the dream with him because maybe he was onto something when he told her what his plans were.

Aarilina got dressed with great haste and when she finished she looked out her window to see it was dusk. It was time to start packing her stuff for the meeting at Humming Forest.

The sunset just before the hills in the far reaches of Aria. The rider wore a hooded cloak over his black armor and entered Adam's field on his horse. The stranger corresponded on his horse from about a quarter of a mile to Animus and his siblings who were planting as they conversed to pass the time.

"Yeah, if I was king I would have seven wives so that everyday would be new," replied Sydney.

"Yes, but how would you get anything done?" asked Aryan.

"He wouldn't, we would be better off with the tyrant we presently have as king," replied Gabriel.

"You guys are demented," interrupted Jada as she suddenly looked up to the figure in the black cloak as he rode in.

The young men stopped shoveling to plant and looked up to the stranger. "I'm here to deliver a letter for a young man by the name of Animus," said the man as pulled off his hood to reveal his brown hazel eyes and hair to match with a few strains of hair that were white. He looked at all the faces before him and finally one of them stepped out.

"I'm Animus."

The messenger handed the envelope to Animus and turned around on his horse to ride away. Animus watched the rider disappear into the distance and opened up the letter to see who it was from then smiled as he read it silently.

Sydney turned his head to Adam who came out of the outhouse that was out of sight behind a group of trees and missed the black rider. Adam became very suspicious when he saw the letter in Animus' hand because nobody delivered mail to them because they were hiding.

"Who is it Animus?" asked Adam suspiciously.

"It's a letter from Aarilina; she wants to meet me at Humming Forest. Father I have to go, she could be in trouble!"

"Animus you're forgetting that you've been exiled from her," replied Adam.

"Trust me," assured Animus. "Everything will be fine."

Animus left to go to the barn and his room and packed up his clothes. He reached under his mattress and pulled out the map to Shadow Mountain and folded it up into his pocket.

Suddenly, Adam walked into his room and looked at him. Animus knew that his father had protected him all these years, but he had to do this on his own.

"Don't try to stop me, I'm not going to listen to you," said Animus.
"I'm not, I just wanted to say good luck and be careful," he replied.
Animus looked at his father and the two hugged each other. Adam nodded his head and slapped his hand on his son's back.
"Go for it, son."

Dear Animus ,
   My love,

I want to see you and long to be in your arms. I miss your gentle fingers caressing upon my lips and body. Every time you touch me it sets my heart on fire and I can't diffuse it. I think about you constantly and can never get you out of my mind.

Father has someone watching over me. Everywhere I go I'm compelled to turn around to see who it is. Every time I do, there is nobody there. Father has threatened to put bars on my window if he finds out I am seeing you, but that won't stop me. He hopes to keep us a part, but it only makes me want you even more. Father is a fool and does not know what love is. You were right about us, and nobody can destroy our bond.

The only way I can see you is if I leave tonight. Meet me in Humming Forest. Please be careful ! Father won't hesitate to put you to your death and keep me a prisoner in my own heart.
Love,

Aarilina

After sundown there was hardly any light to see where the path was. Animus walked around Humming Forest and was looking for Aarilina. Humming Forest was about a mile away from the first gate and wall, north of the castle. The shadows along the branches and lower stumps were dark and creepy, but Animus continued to walk through the forest. He could feel anxiety fill his veins as a light tingly feeling went up and down his back. The farm boy looked around after hearing the hoot of the owl and the chirps of the birds. He remembered that this was where he met Aarilina, but she was nowhere to be seen. Suddenly, there was a loud commotion, a giant net was thrown on him and Animus found himself captured by a group of men.

"Look at what we found," said one of the men holding a torch.

"It looks like we have trespasser," laughed another.

"I'm not a trespasser let me go!" exclaimed Animus as he tried to rip the net apart.

"What is your name boy?" asked another one of the men.

"We've got the right one Prince Tusk," said another one of the other soldiers .

"My name is Animus and I'm with the princess."

Prince Tusk looked at the young man with a torch for Animus to see him and then at the men he was with and nodded. Animus recognized Prince Tusk as the one who delivered the letter to him.

"This is the one we're looking for, the fool who is in love with the princess. King Owen will be pleased," assured the prince as he watched Animus' eyes widened and realized he had been tricked.

The men charged and kicked Animus in the head and stomach. The peasant felt the back of his head crack from a piece of metal as his eardrum began ringing. He felt blood soak in his hair and the pain was tremendous as he was dragged off from the woods to the castle.

The princess packed up the last of her things and dreamed of where they would kiss and touch each other in the night. She smiled with the thought and ran to open the door but gasped in fear.

"Father," she stammered and continued. "I was just coming to see you."

"If you were coming down to see me why would you need this?" he asked while looking at her small bag next to the door.

The princess looked at the bag and then at her father who looked angry. He slowly walked into her room as she receded back. His eyes locked onto hers and then she realized who had been reading her diary.

"The letter I wrote in my diary, you read it," she said as her voice began to break.

"You used me as a trophy, humiliated me and snooped in my room all because I'm in love with Animus," said Princess Aarilinus as she stopped moving backwards and gathered her courage.

"I've read everything and I must say you disgrace me. I've been an honorable, obedient, forthright father and hold a kingdom made of gold," he replied.

"A kingdom made of gold? That's all you care about? This image you see me as; a beautiful queen holding a sword and shield. To be wise, stern and bestow justice throughout the kingdom," she declared.

"You know what I want you to do," replied the king.

"Rules and images of you surround me. That's all that matters to you! I shatter this image into a million pieces!" she exclaimed. There was absolute silence as the two looked at each other, "father, it is only love, what is the harm in that?"

King Owen was taken back and the question reminded him of what her mother once said to him, "the harm is him! The thought of a peasant ruling the kingdom is like stabbing me a thousand times, it sickens me like a person eating maggots. The mere sight of a peasant ruling will destroy me, the royal family, and will leave me in disgrace!"

"Is that all you care about? The heart of yours and not the heart of mine?" she cried.

"Think about all the good I've done for you! I put all my energy into helping you choose a good man out of the five princes who are worthy of your love and able to protect you from anyone who will one day kill you! I've done everything for you, I've protected you, read to you when you were a little girl, fed you chocolate and brought you along when I had dealings with other kingdoms. I didn't do all this so you could marry some stupid peasant, with the intelligents of a dog. Is this how you repay my love?" shouted King Owen.

Princess Aarilinus trembled in tears as she watched the king calm down and for a few minutes there was silence and this scared the princess. She started shaking her head back and forth slowly realizing there was going to be no end to this fight.

"Are you going to kill me father?" she began slowly. "Like you killed my bodyguard?"

"I have no other alternative, but to kill Animus and lock you in the High Tower." "You captured Animus?" she asked.

"Yes I have and to prove it I will let you see him. I'll let him live if you choose to marry one of the five suitors who are set to retrieve the mask."

"You can't do that!" she cried.

"Oh I can," began King Owen slowly as he continued. "And I will, you must decide what you will do and I will let Animus go after your marry someone else."

"There is no proof that you will keep your word is there?" she asked.

"You will just have to trust me," said King Owen as he smiled.

"Trust?" said Aarilina. "You don't know the meaning of the word. Trusting you is like reaching my hand into the mouth of a tiger to retrieve one of my bracelets."

"Then I will show how honorable I am by revealing Animus. Is that not trustworthy enough?" he asked.

"No, releasing him is trusting that you won't kill him."

"You give me little choice, but I will let you speak to him and set him free only if you promise to end your relationship and by doing so you must tell him that you don't love him, humiliate him and tell him you don't want to see him again. I don't want you leaving or I'll kill him, if you refuse to marry one of the men I've selected, I'll kill him. If you raise your voice in a manner that displeases me, I'll kill him. Do we understand each other?"

Princess Aarilinus wiped her eyes with her hands and nodded, "yes."

King Owen and Princess Aarilinus stepped down to the dungeon followed by five soldiers. It was dark, wet and because of the harsh coldness the princess snugged deep into her red cloak to keep warm. Prisoners, both men and women grouped up to the cells like dogs begging for food. She walked past them and felt their stares and pleads. "Princess please, help me!" cried one man after the other.

"Your highness please help me, I implore you I haven't stolen anything!" replied another.

The sad eyes and dirty faces of men and women dominated the young lady's mind who wanted to help them, but couldn't. They were treated like animals and the king ordered them to be silent. Tears filled her eyes as she tried to ignore them in order to see Animus.

They reached another chamber of the dungeon where the insane people were held and the king unlocked the gate to enter a long corridor of cells. They walked past cells with fewer inmates this time they glared at the princess like a piece of meat.

"Hey girl, want to have some fun," grinned an old feeble man from inside the cell.   "You're the one who did this to me" yelled a crazy old man.

Then an ugly lady reached for Aarilina through the bars with a blind eye, "come to me my dear, I'll make your pretty!"

Princess Aarilinus looked at the lady who laughed like a witch. Then she saw another man who was young and stuttered to himself. His face was dirty and he had eyes of a madman as he glared at her. Goosebumps covered her arms as though there was a cool draft along the path, but she was scared.

Finally, they reached the cell where they saw a sad young man sitting alone and looking at the floor. Aarilina could hardly believe that it was Animus because his face had stains of blood and he looked like he was beaten up. It was days since they kissed and it would be the last time she would ever see him again but she had to do this, to save him. The king nodded his head to the princess and she stepped into the cage led by a soldier as her father kept out of sight.

"Aarilina!" gasped Animus with a smile as he shot up from the floor and suddenly realized he was restrained by chains. The peasant looked into the eyes of his love and saw a cold stare from her, a look that made him lower than the insects.

"Why are you looking at me like that?" he asked.

"Animus I've found someone else. You were nothing but a resolute, a play-pretty of my amusement and I want you to disappear and never show your face again!" she exclaimed.

King Owen started laughing as he listened to his daughter insult Animus. The soldiers laughed with him and the king covered his mouth to keep quiet.

"But," cried Animus as he watched her give him a cold look, his lips trembled and his eyes welled up with tears.   "What about all the love we shared?"

"It means nothing, your nothing but a joke. I'm in love with Prince Tusk so don't bother coming back to show your face!" she screamed as she watched a tear fall on Animus' cheek and he watched her turn her back on him.

Before another word could be spoken the princess left and so did the soldier. Aarilina stood down the corridor near the junction of the next set of cells, away from Animus' cage as tears streamed down her cheeks and she cried. She experienced a pain in her chest that was never felt before. The king stopped laughing and tried to act natural around her.

"Your highness," said the first soldier. "Are you going to be alright?"

"Go, leave me," she sobbed and the knight left her alone and she balled her eyes out, "forgive me Animus, please forgive me." Aarilina cried in a whisper and hit the wall with her fist as hard as she could before leaving the dungeons.

King Owen walked in the cell where Animus was as though nothing was wrong and glared at Animus. The king sneered at him as the group of five soldiers walked in and stared at Animus coldly.

"You see, I always win and you will be remembered as the fool."

"Those are mighty words you use as a spoiled child!" yelled Animus.

"What do you mean?" asked King Owen.

"You can't even cure the happiness for your own daughter."

"You think you make my daughter happy? She pities you."

"My father, Adam Brokenheart was right about you."

"Adam Brokenheart" said King Owen as he remembered. "So you're the son of Adam Brokenheart," continued the king as he raised his voice. "I didn't know your last name and now the prophecy makes sense!"

"You can't even help yourself! After your wife died you have become a monster. Why do you think you've not re-married!" shouted Animus as he watched King Owen turn red

"Silence!" exclaimed King Owen and he charged up to the peasant with his face up to Animus.

"Don't you dare talk about my wife!" yelled the king as saliva spit in Animus' face and he watched Animus take a deep breath.

"Throw the boy to the Dark Wolves!" King Owen yelled as he revealed a sneer and watched Animus' mouth drop.

Animus felt his heart beat faster just as his eyes widened and he could feel his limbs being ripped apart. Without another word Animus' chains were unbound by the king's soldiers and watched another soldier pull a lever and Animus fell through a trap door. The peasant felt the rush of air hit his face while hearing the wind rush against his ears.

Suddenly, with a big swap that sounded like a bag of sand, Animus hit the ground and raised his head and he could hear the ringing in his ears. A few minutes went by and Animus got up from the sand. The young man groaned while looking around as he felt stinging on his forehead and had a nose bleed. Animus took care of his nose bleed until it stopped and then he looked around. He saw he was in a big chamber with huge rocks and bricks as walls. There were boulders around him, sand and a lot of skeleton remains. He grabbed a torch from the wall to have a look around and escape.

Animus heard a strange flapping sound similar to a bird was heard and turned to see five hideous creatures in front of him. They looked like wolves and were about the size of antelopes with large black bat like wings that were about two meters in length. The creatures folded their wings back along their torso and looked at Animus with their red eyes. Animus stared at the monsters as they walked towards him revealing their sharp teeth and talons.

"Please don't eat me," Animus whispered to himself.

"Eat you?" asked one of the creatures with a deep voice.

"Yes, you are the Dark Wolves are you not?" asked the peasant.

"Yes we are," answered the dark wolf with a deep voice. "We are hungry for flesh and fear."

"Then what are you waiting for?" asked Animus.

"This boy wants us to eat him," laughed one of the other creature's.

"We eat only the ones who fear us. You do not react the way the others have. I smell no fear from you," replied the the presumed leader as he continued to stare at Animus and began walking around the him.

"Tell me your name boy?" spoke one of the other creatures with a higher pitched voice than the leader.

"My name is Animus."

"Animus the king?" asked another.

"No just Animus, now you tell me your names!" demanded the farm boy suspiciously.

"We do not answer to demands," growled the leader and he purposely blew air into the back of the young man's head. Animus turned his head quickly and stared at the monster.

"Tell him our names. For all we know he probably is the one who will free us," replied one of the other dark wolves with a semi deep voice.

"Shut up Shepherd or I will have you thrown out of the circle," barked the leader as he turned his attention back to Animus.

"Very well I will tell you my name, but only if you tell us why you're down here?"

Animus looked at the leader and took a deep breath, "I'm in love with the princess, I was thrown down here against my will and was tricked by her father when I was going to retrieve the mask of Furrengee."

"Mask you say," said another voice.

"He's the one who will free us, we must help him only then will the spell be broken," said another.

"Shut up!" yelled the leader.

"So who are you?" demanded Animus.

"We're the Dark Wolves; I am Rampant, The Black Sorcerer of Fire and Darkness," he said and he gestured the other Dark Wolves to introduce themselves.

"I am Earman, The Blue Sorcerer of Air and Sound."

"I am Lore, The Silver Sorcerer of Water and Stone."

"I am Shepherd, The White Sorcerer of Trees and Light."

"I am Malice, The Gold Sorcerer of Soul and Possession."

"You're on a quest to proclaim the mask, but you must promise you will free us," insisted Rampant.

"Why don't you just fly out of here?" asked Animus.

"If we did that do you think we would be standing here talking to you?" asked Malice.

"We were put under a spell by a master of evil. We have been locked in our form for thousands of years and we would remain like this forever unless we were set free by the one who wore the mask of Furrengee," said Rampant.

"How did this happen?" asked Animus.

"Ten thousand years ago we were the rulers of the first five kingdoms and we were deceived by an evil wizard. This wizard imprisoned us in the form you see us now. The wizard sought pity upon us and predicted for our release that the spell would be broken if a man named Animus set us free. This man as king would set us free to unite the five kingdoms and bring peace and prosperity to the land," declared Earman.

"So you believe that this person is me?" asked Animus.

"It has been predicted for ten thousand years and there is order for every prophecy," answered Malice.

"Don't you see, if we leave this prison our true form will return as it was thousands of years ago, permanently!" exclaimed Lore.

"Who was the wizard that imprisoned you?" asked Animus.

"We don't remember his name," answered Rampant.

"He was child like, with a feminine face. He was tall and bold with silver streaks that ran through his whitish blonde hair," added Earman.

"What was his name?" repeated Animus.

"It was a wizard named Xaggess who imprisoned us," replied Shepherd, reluctantly.

"What has this got to do with me? I want to win Aarilina back," replied Animus but then he remembered what she said to him.

"Win her heart you shall when you set us free. It has been foreseen in the prophecy that you stand with us to unite the kingdoms and end all wars," grinned Malice.

"With our help you could be the most powerful king in the land that no adversary will dare oppose," continued Rampant.

"I don't think putting pressure and intimidation on the neighboring kingdoms is something that will persuade them to join," replied Animus.

"It's the most perfect idea! Your enemies will surrender and kneel before you as cowards. We could teach you our power and help you become a sorcerer. You would be invincible and capable of doing so much good as we had. It's your destiny to set us free and take your place as king of Aria," declared Lore.

"I don't believe I will need your help after I possess the mask of Furrengee. It will enable me to be the king that Aria has needed for a long time. I will always be the man that Aarilina sees before her and have no desire for such power," said Animus.

"The mask will not give you all the power that we will bestow upon you, young lord," replied Earman.

"Yes, imagine having control over the weak minds of men to unite the land against the rise of evil," continued Malice.

"As well as the power to control night and day," persuaded Rampant.

"I don't know," stammered Animus as he tried to think. "I don't know if I can do this."

"Will you set us free?" asked Shepherd.

"I can't set you free if I'm in this prison with no escape," replied Animus.

"There is a way out," said Rampant as he gestured his head to the ceiling. "There is a window near the dropped door where your king disposes his victims for us to feed on."

"Our last victim was Edward Bobbit and he was tasty," grinned Malice as he watched Animus look at him with a dreadful look.

"Is the window barred?" asked Animus as he looked at Rampant.

"The bars are bent enough for you to fit through," answered Rampant.

"How do I get up there?" asked Animus as he looked up to the ceiling.

"We will fly you up there, but before we do that you must promise to free us," ordered Rampant.

"After I have retrieved the mask and rescued my beloved Aarilina I will free you for sparing my life, but I do not ask for anything from you except your silence to live your own life without involving yourselves in humanity," said Animus.

"Agreed," they all answered.

"Climb on my back and I will help you reach the exit," ordered Rampant.

Animus slid on the beast's back and felt his soft fur and wings as they moved up and down. They ascended and Animus could see the barred window. He grabbed hold of one of the bars with one hand and then grabbed the other as he swung himself through the opening.

Animus looked around after squeezing through the exit to see where he was. The peasant knew he was just outside the castle; he carefully avoided the soldiers, climbed over the castle gate and snuck past the soldiers to get through the second and first gate. He sprinted through the woods just as he saw a horse with a saddle and a soldier urinating in the bushes. Animus looked around and found a large rock that was the size of a grapefruit and threw it at the soldier and hit him in the head, knocking him out.

The young man climbed on the horse and hoped that he wouldn't get bucked off. Without a word Animus shook the reins and the horse whinnied as they charged though the forest to Shadow Mountain.

The moon revealed itself in the night sky. Animus felt the cool breeze hit his face upon the humidity. He was at Shadow Mountain and unfolded the map to see how he could enter and navigate through without endangering his life.

Shadow Mountain was a carved face of a skull into the base of the mountain that was produced thousands of years ago. It camouflaged the citadel that was inside the mountain. The temple, inside Shadow Mountain, was timeless and forged by rock and stone unfolding in and out as a huge triangular pyramid. Animus didn't know how long the temple existed, but heard it was built prior to the carved skull and was the resting place for Furrengee's mask. Furrengee, the greatest warrior that ever lived was written in story and legend. The legend and source of power of the mask involved the dead warriors who wore the mask during battle.

Animus looked at the entries on the back of the map, written by his father, which revealed that anyone who entered the citadel. The elders spoke of Shadow

Mountain as a place where goblins kidnapped little children years ago to sacrifice them.

Animus got off his steed and turned around to look at his horse, "I wish you could go where I'm going friend, but you should be set free."

The horse nudged its head into Animus' face and nickered just as the peasant laughed. He took off the saddle and reins while thinking about his challenge. After he was finished he gave the horse a quick slap and it galloped away.

After minutes of thinking, Animus began walking to Shadow Mountain. Every step of the way the farm boy had fear of what would happen to him. Animus walked inside the skeleton mouth of Shadow Mountain and saw the torches already lit. This struck the farm boy as odd and he wondered if someone was already here. He continued through a long corridor with a torch he took off from the side of the wall.

In the distance of about twenty feet he came to the sight of the temple. It looked creepy and evil, but he continued on until he was able to touch it. He examined the temple and it looked almost bigger than the castle of Aria and he slowly touched the rough brick wall with his fingers with the torch in his hand. He was looking for a secret lever to open the secret passageway as it was described on the piece of paper. Suddenly, Animus felt a weak impression in the brick wall and pushed it in and an opening in the wall revealed itself that was the size big enough for a person to fit through.

The farm boy walked inside and felt the intense humidity as though he were inside a volcano and began to perspire quickly. Big bats, the size of buzzards, flew past him with their high pitch noises and one of them attacked him bit biting his face. Animus screamed in fear because he had never seen bats that big and struck the bat as hard as he could with his hand.

It was dark, stale and a long corridor of torches filled long spaces. Animus could barely see in the gloom of smoke and he wiped the sweat that dripped from his forehead. The sight of skeletons and statues holding torches made Animus' stomach turn. The immense space of darkness in between each sight of torches made it difficult to know what to expect. His father was right about the temple and knew it was going to be difficult to get the mask. Animus, suddenly heard a grinding noise from behind and turned, waiving the torch to see the secret doorway had closed.

Sweat perspired from his forehead again and he continued to wipe it off as he turned around to continue down the tunnel. Animus didn't like the feeling of being trapped in the temple and thought about Aarilina and the way she treated him. He was sad because he fantasized about their wedding and how great it would be. Maybe if he got the mask she would love him again and the hurtful things she said would go away.

The peasant took a deep breath and wiped the sweat from his face as he opened up the map and read the entries his father wrote. He learned that the warriors who entered the front entrance would endure worse than when he entered the secret doorway.

The farm boy pulled his hair over his ears and turned the map around to see what was ahead. He could hear the sound of water dripping from the sweat of the ceiling while biting his lip to read what details laid ahead.

He looked over the map that showed the way through a maze of tunnels marked with blood, marking all the traps in the citadel. A feeling of hopelessness filled such mind as Animus looked ahead of the path and realized that he missed something. The map

revealed there was a cross road up ahead, but he could see the tunnel was going straight ahead. He suddenly walked straight into an invisible barrier and hurt his nose.

Animus made sure that he didn't have a nose bleed and touched the invisible barrier. He touched it with both hands and gently leaned his forehead on it to see through it was a dark long corridor.

The farm boy pulled out the map to see the thick hollow line crossing over that symbolized path. The young man's eyes glared at the dwindling flame of his torch and knew that he needed a torch or fuel for his fire. Animus ripped his old, cotton, vest given to him by his grandfather to feed the fire. He wrapped the fabric around the torch and watched with relief as the flame grew.

Animus looked at the map and realized there was a way around the invisible barrier and to the sub level to another chamber. He walked down the stairs and found himself in another corridor.

When he stepped off the last step he noticed a lot of spider webs. Animus suddenly got nervous and walked slowly past them. Each spider web he passed was bigger and he felt his muscles tighten up and walked slowly past them. Every step of the way, Animus held the folded map and looked around for whatever creature that would appear before him. Suddenly, he was caught in a giant spider web but he managed to pull himself through to stay on the path.

 He stopped in shock as he waived his torch to see the skeleton remains of animals the size of sheep dogs. The peasant wiped the sweat from his brow and looked at the map to see there were dozens of traps ahead of his path. Animus continued onward; walking carefully in the dark with the torch. Then something in the distance was crawling on all fours like a dog made its way in his path and he heard it make grunting noise. It looked like a rat and Animus whistled at the creature ahead of him hoping it was a dog. Animus kept moving ahead but then screamed in terror when it moved towards him and tried to attack him. He could see clearly now that it was a rat, a very large rat.

"What in Ayana!" exclaimed Animus as his eyes widen to see more rats, the size of large dogs, walking towards him. From the path ahead of him.

The rats looked at him with their beady eyes and they licked their lips to attack him. They hissed at Animus and moved in closer as the young man swung his torch at them, to keep them from eating him alive. One rat jumped at Animus and bit his arm, but was pushed and kicked back, burned by Animus' torch. The rats heard the screaming of their fellow rat and smelled the burning meat and then they retreated back through the holes in the walls.

Animus continued to stoop and walk through the tunnel until he walked into a large room. He looked around to see it was filled with boulders, statues and a stream of fire that was lit on three ledges along the walls and four corners of the room. He opened the map after taking a few minutes to look around and noticed that it wasn't hot like it was in the tunnel, but it was warm. He felt a strange unrest in the air, the room looked like an arena for a challenge, *but what was the challenge?* Animus was relieved that he wouldn't have to worry about giant rats attacking him, but something caught his attention. Goosebumps covered his arms and he knew something was wrong.

He looked to see a silver sword, bow and arrows, morning star, javelin, and a

shield which were held in the hands of the statues. Animus moved quickly to grabbed each one and realized that the weapons were shiny and hadn't been used before. The six foot long javelin had a button that worked like a lever which could be reduced in size to a foot long cylinder. The shield was made from a strange material that was very light just as the sword was but was very strong. The morning star had a button on the handle so that the ball and pins would become a flail. Animus looked around at the empty chamber and gathered the weapons. He looked at the map when suddenly he saw a bright light emerge from inside a tunnel ahead of him and entered the doorway.

Animus followed the long path until the source of light could be seen, which led to the next chamber. Animus pushed in on an indention on the handle which was a button for the chain on the ball to recoil the morning star into his belt. He slid the morning star into his belt and pulled out his sword. His legs twitch from the excitement when he got the weapons but he felt so tired.

He was in a garden that looked similar to the Clandestine Garden that was lit by a sphere the size of a cantaloupe. Animus took another step while sliding his sword back into its sheath when he realized there was no danger and unraveled the map.

After reading it, he realized the clue was a trapped door to escape. The objective was to hit the energy sphere while it remained suspended in one spot and the trapped door would reveal itself. Animus put the map back in his back pocket after finding out the chamber was home to a beast called the Poison Widow. He looked around at the beautiful trees and plants to see fruits that looked really good. He was hungry and thirsty and couldn't remember the last time he ate. The smell of sugar and honey made his stomach whine and he resisted the temptation to eat the fruits.

Animus walked closer to the glowing ball as its pulse of light mesmerized his eyes. The snap of a twig got his adrenaline pumping with each step on the grass. He gripped the handle of his sword while it was in its sheath as the hair on the back of his neck stood up. He could hear something move along the ground from behind him and suddenly felt something grab and pull his ankle quickly, thrusting him flat on his back.

Animus pulled out his sword and cut the vine that was dragging him. The farm boy looked straight ahead and his eyes widened in terror to the beast before him with its tongue attached to his ankle.

It was the Poison Widow thundering on all fours like an ape just as it was described in his father's notes. It looked like a giant red tomato with thorns and flowers sticking out with a giant beak like mouth in the front.

The beast stood up on its brown stump hind legs; unleashed a roar at Animus then closed its mouth half way while its tongue gripped Animus' ankle. Animus felt himself getting dragged closer to the creature and kept striking the monster's tongue with his sword. The Poison Widow screeched while opening its mouth and kept pulling the farm boy towards it. After another thrust of the sword the Widow Plant retracted its tongue back into its mouth.

Animus held his shield in front of his body just as the beast shot thorns at him. The sound of thorns hit Animus' shield and dropped to the ground a few feet on either side of him as he pushed his sword back into his sheath.

The peasant reached for his belt behind his back and rose quickly with the morning star as he carefully swung the ball and chain in circles. He pushed the indention to activate the pins and the chain came out of the top of the cylinder followed by the pins that emerged out. The Widow Plant snarled as Animus struck it again and again sending pieces of its flesh upon the grass.

Animus kept swinging, realizing that he could hit the beast from a distance with the flail without getting hurt. After hitting it from a distance, he charged at the Poison Widow drawing strength as he charged and held onto the flail as he hit it as hard as he could. The farm boy let out a battle cry as saliva dripped from his teeth. Animus struck the creature's tongue with his morning star that shot from its mouth and heard the beast howl in pain. The peasant resumed his stature to get leverage so that he wouldn't lose his balance and struck the beast again with his morning star, but because he he hit it so hard the weapon was stuck.

The Poison Widow unleashed a roar in pain and charged as it thrust its stump like fist at Animus just before he raised his shield to block the blow. The force threw Animus back ten feet onto the ground and flat on his back. The peasant raised his head to see the beast snarl angrily like a gorilla and leaped in the air to jump on top of him.

Animus pulled out his javelin that was fastened behind his belt and pushed an indented button, which made the small stick grow to its original length with sharp points on either side. He pointed it at the creature that was charging and watched as the javelin entered the Poison Widow's mouth and exited out the other side.

The Poison Widow screamed in pain as Animus moved quickly and pressed the button on the javelin and it receded to a foot long and Animus moved his agile body under the creature's torso to reclaim the flail. The beast let out a scream as Animus pulled out the weapon and the beast tried to strike Animus, but failed.

The peasant thrust the morning star as hard as he could and watched the ball in chain detach from the long handle and embed itself back into the Poison Widow's exterior. Once again, it got stuck in the creature, but this time the creature grabbed the chain and Animus up in the air, over its head and back on the ground. The Poison Widow had plunged him into the grass and he felt pain in his torso.

Animus raised his head up from the grass and felt the bleeding from his upper lip and a gash on his forehead as well as the pain in his ribs. He rose up from the ground with his aching limbs. He heard the sound of snarling come from the beast as it chomped its teeth together like it was laughing at him. Something didn't make since because the creature didn't attack him right away which made the peasant come to the conclusion that it was waiting until he would be too tired to fight.

Animus pulled out his bow drawing out an arrow from its sleeve that was on his back and aimed at the beast's mouth before it charged at him. Animus fired again and slid the bow over his shoulder. He pulled out his sword and stepped aside as fast as he could just before the creature ran past him then he took his sword and cut into the monster's flesh.

"In the name of the Burning Bush, Xaggess and Jetsu would you die!" Animus exclaimed as he grabbed the handle of the morning star and pulled it from the creature's flesh. The beast howled in pain and a strange red liquid dripped from its body. It turned around at Animus and let out a strange sound that sounded like it was laughing at him again.

Animus clutched the golden handle of his sword as he took a couple of deep breaths to re-cooperate. Then Animus remembered from the notes of his father that hitting the glowing sphere was connected to defeating the Poison Widow. How could he have been this stupid, thought Animus. All this time trying to kill it and all he had to do was strike the pulsing sphere that he saw earlier.

Animus quickly took out his bow and arrow, pulled the string back with an arrow loaded as he aimed it at the sphere pulsing with light. The farm boy felt a rush of adrenaline run up his shoulders as he felt the tension of the string with his fingers. He released the string and the arrow shot through the air and into the glowing sphere. Animus turned his head to hear the Poison Widow unleash a horrible scream in agony. Fire burst through the creatures flesh and after a few minutes passed the beast collapsed to the ground and blew apart into pieces of charcoal.

Animus suddenly heard the sounds of gears throughout the chamber and a trapped door opened up under the grass, revealing a square hole. It revealed itself from under the pulsing ball of light and the peasant took a deep breath of relief. He walked to the secret passageway and slid the bow and arrow over his shoulder as he placed his weapons back into their place.

The doors began to close and he took one last look at the Widow Plant that was now destroyed. He felt a rush of air against his cheeks and the sweat continued to drip from his forehead. He found himself on another path that led to the next chamber.

The tunnel was pitch black and Animus reached with his left hand in front of him and touched the walls with his right hand. He felt pain in his joints and face from his fight with the Widow Plant. He could still taste the blood on his lips and feel the stinging on his forehead. It felt like a flashback of when the king's knights caught him at Humming Forest and beat him bloody.

He stumbled in the dark after nearly tripping over a rock and he felt the hot air shoot up from the cracks below. Animus was angry for the way he was treated by the king and the princess. *Why am I doing this? She doesn't love me anymore he thought to himself. Why should I get the mask and save this person who misled me when she's nothing, but a spoiled girl.* Animus thought angrily. The farm boy wiped his tears and took a deep breath as he looked at a pool of lava ahead of him.

Animus kneeled close to the edge, just before the cat walk and directed the torch to light it and pulled back to see the new flame begin to grow. The young man looked around the tunnel with his torch that went straight ahead and moved ahead.

He smelled death around him as he feared the worst of what was to come. Animus rose up to catch the edge of his back against the wall and felt something large crawling on him. The peasant quickly knocked it down with his hand and turned to see what it was. It was a tarantula the size of an apple and it ran away from him to a hole in the wall and disappeared.

Animus took each step slowly as he waved the torch around to be sure he wouldn't get attacked. Suddenly, a giant tarantula charged at him from a large hole in the wall. The farm boy pulled out his sword and swung it quickly at the eight legged creature that opened its jaws to devour him. He quickly ran back and then turned around to thrust the spider with the torch and sword. The tarantula made a loud squeal that sounded like a scream and scurried back into the large hole in the wall.

The peasant felt his knees tremble and goosebumps covered his arms. He knew there would be more giant rats and tarantulas waiting for him. He could already see pictures of his corpse being eaten and ripped apart by the rats.

After the long walk down the corridor of statues and skeletons he came to another chamber long and narrow. It led to a catwalk that looked silver and below the cat walk was more bubbling lava. The chamber was circular and the walls were gold in color and a white light shined from an opening on the ceiling to a pillow on a ledge that had an object on it, which was the mask.

Animus' eyes widened when he saw the mask on the pillow, on top of the alter made of brick. He took a step forward and suddenly a large sphere with spikes attached to a chain swung to hit him from a hidden trap door on the wall. Animus backed away and watched it swing back and forth and then back to the opening that was inside the wall.

The farm boy was confused and frustrated; how was he going to get the mask when there would be more of these traps to prevent him from succeeding? Animus opened the map again to see if there were any clues. He looked on the back of the map to see a composition was written and Animus read it a loud.

only one that is brave to walk across the bridge
must not only risk the hearts of others, but his own
and walk across the bridge with his eyes closed
for it is not the fallens that are shown
but your own reflection that have the traps rigged

Animus was in deep thought and looked around the chamber, the words stuck in his head. He looked around the gold exterior of the chamber and the silver catwalk. He felt with his heart and saw one thing in common with all of them. They showed a reflection of him and realized that was what set the traps. *How is closing my eyes going to get me across safely?* Animus thought to himself. He took off his weapons and set them near the entrance then cleared his mind and took a deep breath while looking at the path before him. He trusted himself with his eyes closed and took two steps upon the catwalk.

As Animus walked across the catwalk, his mind began to wander to the times as a child crying out of fear of the dark. He was scared of the dark and needed someone to help guide him through. It was his father who helped him through when he was a child.

"Imagine yourself with nothing to fear in the dark and you will free yourself of the dark," Animus said as h remembered that was what his father would say.

"I'm scared of the dark," said Animus to himself as he remembered and continued. "Animus, the darkness can't hurt you, it can only deter you from finding your way."

Animus felt a wave of confidence build inside of him as he imagined the catwalk and at the end of the silver walkway was Aarilina with the mask in her hands. He could see her long hair stretch past the front of her waist and looking at him with a smile. He knew what she said hurt him, but he wondered if she lied to protect him from her father.

He continued to walk with his eyes closed and could hear the bubbling sound of the lava pit below and felt the humidity perspire his body with sweat. Before he knew it he bumped into the alter and felt the pillow. Animus opened his eyes and covered them from the light above and slowly traced his fingers over the smooth textured metal mask. The lips were embossed with dark stone marble that had been pushed and encased from the fire of its creation. The lips were pushing upwards in an angry look of a warrior and the outside of the eyes were carved smoothly along the cheeks as the nose stuck out abruptly.

Animus smiled when he saw visions in a dream like state of past warriors from long ago, who fought to the death for the woman they loved. He could hear and see them, in light and in blue silhouette, fighting monsters and kissing the woman they loved. Animus let go of the mask and felt his heartbeat faster. The impression was strong that he almost lost control of his feelings. Animus took a deep breath and touched the mask again to see more. Suddenly, an image of Furrengee entered Animus' dream like state and he looked exactly as he remembered him from the stories and illustrations. Animus awoke from his trance, turned his head to see the warrior named Furrengee, without the mask over his face, who towered over him at seven feet tall with long black hair and smiled at him. He crossed his arms as Animus' mouth dropped in shock and looked up at the giant. Animus took his hands off the mask wondering and hoping he wasn't hallucinating.

"You found the courage to seek my mask, just as your father had and he was worthy. You have been chosen Animus to use the mask for Princess Aarilinus," said Furrengee in a deep voice as his strong brown eyes looked into Animus' eyes with confidence and assurance.

"How did you know that I needed it for Aarilina?"

"I have seen your mind and know your dreams," said Furrengee as he continued.

"The princess needs you. Despite what she said to you to hurt you. She is in trouble and needs you to save her. You must go to her, Animus. Everything depends on it."

"I will, I promise," declared Animus with a nod as he wiped his eyes while feeling the weight of the world on his shoulders and shook Furrengee's large hand.

Animus had never felt so important and it took his breath away. He watched Furrengee dissipate out of thin air in front of him and the light from above disappeared, leaving light from the lava. The peasant gently removed the mask from the pillow and put it over his face. At first, it felt like an ordinary mask then he heard thousands of voices. The mask illuminated the room with a brilliant white light and Animus felt a change come over him.

His body became muscular; his hair became black and grew past his shoulders and parts of his bangs grew past the eyes of the mask. White light broke through his body while a black, shiny, armored vest emerged out of his skin and then his limbs were covered in black armor. Animus felt a black, leather cape sink knee level, behind his legs and looked at himself through the mask. He could see countless men in his mind who looked ghostly and Animus realized that they had worn the mask and were the same people he saw earlier. Animus turned to the catwalk and picked up his weapons before exiting the chamber. He walked with confidence and began to increase to seven feet tall, realizing nothing could stop him.

Deep inside Shadow Mountain the legend was reborn. The power of invincibility was re-discovered and fueled his ambition as well as his desire for Princess Aarilinus. A fist busted through the mountain quickly and sounded like thunder from a storm. He looked outside the large hole of Shadow Mountain and walked through to see it was night. He walked to a tree with a pile of sticks and brush to set the weapons next to it to hide them from sight. He stood up while his mask reflected the light from the moon, his cape moved slowly when the breeze hit it. The moon was full among the dark blue sky. Suddenly, he used his power to make his body twenty feet in height. The giant made his march and kicked boulders from his path as he felt powerful and beyond the bounds of his enemy, King Owen.

    The princess combed her hair while she soaked in a royal bath of hot water and bubbles. It had been a day since she last saw Animus, it was also her birthday, but she felt lonely. She was imprisoned in the High Tower for trying to escape with Animus. She was ordered to attend the royal ball that evening to dance with the five princes and get to know them before they would proclaim the mask. The ball would have been romantic if Animus was invited, but she felt there was no recourse from her father and she was deeply sad.

    She looked into the mirror, as Jenna took the brush and combed the princess' hair back. Her skin was white like porcelain and she smelled like roses. She shed a tear as she kept thinking about Animus. Jenna stopped what she was doing and left to get some ointment to keep Aarilina's hair conditioned. The princess knew she screwed up with Animus back in the dungeon and that everything was her fault but she did it to save his life.

    The branches of the trees swayed down as the wind blew through the land. Furrengee stepped over trees as he looked at the castle in the far distance and continued his march. The animals ran in different directions, the mice and rabbits ran to take shelter in their homes to avoid being stepped on as the wolves and wildcats did the same. The fiduciaries guided Animus each step of the way to a bridge across the river. The giant took a step upon the bridge and it immediately busted apart because of his weight, causing the giant to fall into the river. After falling feet first into fifteen feet of water the twenty foot giant increased his size to thirty feet and continued the journey.

    Aarilina looked into the mirrors that were around her bath tub. Jenna returned to the princess with the ointment and began to massage it into her hair. She leaned the princess' head back on the pillow and applied a wet towel over her eyes,

    "Rest my dear," whispered Jenna.

    The princess relaxed and felt the warmth of the wet towel over her eyes while Jenna polished her finger nails. Deep inside, the princess was screaming through her mind while thinking about her future without Animus. *Would her life be the same without Animus?* She thought to herself and knew that it wouldn't.

"Jenna," began Aarilina. "If you loved someone so much would you kill yourself to prevent another man from having you?"

"Child what speak is this? In a matter of days you will become queen of the kingdom!"

"Please answer the question, it's important," whispered Aarilina.

"Well I don't know, he would have to mean more to me than life itself. You're not still mad at me for reporting you to your father are you?" asked Jenna, but she didn't get an answer.

That was all Aarilina needed to hear since suicide seemed rational to get revenge with father for taking advantage of her. The handmaiden took off the wet towel from the princess' eyes; helped Aarilina out of the tub, dried her well with a big towel and dressed her with a robe.

"Leave me please, I want to go to sleep," commanded the princess sadly as she turned around to look at the nurse.

"You're not going to do anything reckless are you?" demanded Jenna as she looked at the princess cautiously.

Aarilina smiled, "when a princess asks for space, I don't think it's too much to ask for when someone she loves will no longer be in her life and she wants to remember his smile before she goes to sleep."

"I don't know, you seemed awfully sad at the dance, I think I should remain."

"Don't trouble yourself, I'll be fine," Aarilina continued to smile. "I'm just not used to changes that involve me leading a nation."

Jenna looked at Aarilina for a long time, hesitating to leave her alone, and then smiled, "very well my dear, but the first chance you need council you let me know."

"I will let you know as soon as possible," assured Aarilina as she smiled and watched Jenna leave and closed the door, but that smile diminished to sadness to reflect her empty heart.

Aarilina knew life wouldn't be the same, she would take her life before giving her heart away to a man she didn't love. The princess caressed her chin with her hand and looked hopelessly to the barred window and began to cry. After a few minutes, she removed her robe and slipped into her nightgown while considering to kill herself. She took off her necklace that she always wore and looked at it. It was a clean cut stone in the shape of a heart that had gold trim around it with a red ruby like color that had a magenta colored stone inside of it. She opened up a small metal case and put it inside and then closed the top. She was so angry at her father that she didn't want to wear it again. Wearing the necklace was to much to wear because her father gave it to her a year ago and it belonged to her mother who died because of her and now Animus was gone and she didn't want to be alive. Aarilina blew out the candle on her dresser and looked around at all the shadows that were in the shape of clouds. She walked to her bed, slid under the covers and snuggled in but knew she would have a hard time sleeping.

The giant increased his size to fifty feet and stepped over the first gate. The soldiers and knights that ran out of their small towers to defend the castle, suddenly came to a halt. They lowered their swords in shock and watched the giant walk past, ignoring them. After their shock came to an end and they realized what was going on they attacked, by firing their bows and arrows, crossbows and threw their spears. Furrengee stopped and turned his head to look down on those who fired and ignored them.

Animus remembered as a child how he was belittled and could hear the fiduciaries warning him to not seek revenge because he would risk the consequences. The archers griped their bows and shot their arrows that were lit with fire at the giant presumed to be Furrengee. The arrows could not pierce through Furrengee's armor and fell to the ground or got stuck in the metal crevices. The brave soldiers tried to slay the giant by stabbing his feet and legs with their swords, but it was no use.

Furrengee continued to walk with Animus' heart pumping for the woman he loved. Many of the warriors ran away from the giant and those those that got in the way were accidentally stepped on and he felt no pity for them. Animus didn't mean to step on them, but thankfully the Fiduciaries said and did nothing. They were only concerned with out right offensive attacks.

Aarilina couldn't sleep; she was having a bad feeling that Animus was dead. Her mind was jumbled and she couldn't decide what she wanted out of life, if Animus was dead then she wanted to die. The princess anticipated two different paths for her future if she wasn't able to die. Such a future gave her a haunting question that she would live for her people and give them hope even if she had none. If she would only live for her people and the people she loved then she was already dead. Then she decided in her heart she would marry no other except Animus and she didn't care if it hurt her father. Her lips trembled and her eyes welled up with tears, hoping she was was wrong and that if Animus was alive and she would choose him, but if he wasn't, would she go through with it? Would she die?

It would be arrogance that the king would force her to marry the one who retrieved the mask of Furrengee. He could hear his voice as he declared it to his knights many years ago that she would be more than queen to the kingdom. *She is the most precious thing in the world to me. She will love in my honor and you will fight to keep her.* She remembered it when she was a young girl sneaking behind the shadows to hear what her father was talking about during the secret meetings. It was what she feared more than anything in the world, to marry a man who would treat her as a slave. The thoughts persisted inside her mind as she closed her eyes and began to sniffle and cry. The princess regretted what she said to Animus when she was in the cell and remembered crying her eyes out while feeling the pain in her chest. Saying I love you would have been better than telling him he was a play pretty for her amusement. It was very mean of her to say that.

All was not lost, for Furrengee had stepped over the second gate and was inside the city. The giant walked on the cobblestone path to the castle. He ignored the soldiers who attacked him on his way to the castle when he got to the golden gate he stepped over it and looked at all the towers.

The masked giant looked around to hear screams from the noble women and shouting from the country men who were outside. Furrengee continued to look at the numerous towers and was trying to figure out where the princess would be. Some of the windows were lit while others were dark. He looked through the windows that were lit and none of them held her captive, until he looked up to the highest tower which was higher than him. Animus used the power of the mask to gathered all his strength and grew a hundred feet to match the height of the highest tower, which was the High Tower.

Princess Aarilinus had a dream when she was being given the Culminate Amethyst by her father. She was in the Mid Tower and the day was warm as she realized she was wearing her nicest dress and her hair was done. A hand touched her shoulder and it was warm. When she turned around it was her father, "I have a gift for you."

Aarilina said nothing because she had relived this moment before in her fantasy, "yes."

"This was your mother's, it's the most precious thing I have. She would have wanted you to have it," said her father.

Aarilina woke up and rose up while sitting in bed to feel the wind upon her face from the window. She could see the curtains move in the shadows of the darkness. It pushed strands of her long bangs into her face. She got out of bed and looked at the window that had the bars and let the wind in. Aarilina looked around and felt like she was being watched, but couldn't see through the white curtains to see what it was.

Suddenly, something broke and multiple objects rolled along the wooden floor. Her intuition told her it was the metal bars, but she had a hard time seeing in the dark. Aarilina quietly tiptoed to the corner of the window and leaned up against the wall. With every deep breath of anticipation; goosebumps made their way to the surface of her skin. Princess Aarilinus had never felt so scared and felt the sweat perspire from her face. She turned her head to peek around the corner of the window. Then Aarilina's eyes grew wide after witnessing a giant eye of a mask, the mask of Furrengee.

Hollow and empty they revealed no emotion because it was a mask. A giant hand busted through the window and made a large hole. It was Furrengee who gently grabbed the princess with his hand and brought her outside the tower to see a hundred feet below would be her death if she fell. Aarilina screamed and felt the giant's hand surround her body.

Furrengee walked away from the tower as he lowered his height from a hundred feet back to fifty feet and closed his hand around the princess to protect her. The soldiers regrouped and fired at the giant with their bows and arrows. Furrengee held the princess carefully as though she was made of glass and Animus didn't want to lose her to the mad men below. Every arrow was ignored and every spear thrown at him whether it hit him or missed was forgotten.

The soldiers engaged the catapults with steelies lit with fire to kill the giant and save the princess. In Animus' mind he could feel the hits from the fireballs and wanted to step on them, but was once again warned to not fall into temptations. Animus moved quickly to the second gate and stepped over and was now in the city.

The fireballs flew through the air and collided into the middle of the giant's back. Furrengee turned to see where they came from and saw numerous catapults shooting more fireballs at him. Animus moved through the city quickly and carefully but had to deal with soldiers shooting at him.

Animus knew he couldn't do anything physically, but knew he could backfire the negative energy onto those who were attacking him and make them suffer. Furrengee raised his right hand in front of his mouth, with his hand flat and blew. He made a blowing sound like a light breeze, which was a curse.

Aarilina held onto the mighty chest armor of Furrengee while watching the battle carry over from the top of his hand. Furrengee turned around to continue the long journey to the first gate and watched the archers, before him, shoot their arrows loaded with fire. The arrows stuck deep into his chest but the giant wiped them with his hand like bread crumbs. A fireball flew through the air and hit the giant in the back of the head. Furrengee turned around and held his hand out to catch all the fireballs. He clenched his hand tightly and crushed the steelies and threw pieces of the debris at the soldiers which made the men stop and pick up diamonds. Furrengee watched them throw their weapons down, to kneel and picked up the diamonds like greedy beggars. The giant turned around and continued the march to the first gate.

Furrengee stepped over the gate with a simple stride. He was now in the forest; the jack rabbits and squirrels ran away from the giant's path to take cover in the woods. He was strong and powerful while slowly reducing his size to twenty feet so that he could blend in with the trees.

"Come on he's getting away," declared one of the knights to the greedy soldiers picking up the diamonds. A soldier jumped to his armored steed loaded with every weapon imaginable. Other knights loaded another steely into the catapult and were preparing to light it on fire.

The flickered light of fire streamed from their torch as they were about to cut it. Suddenly, the steelie exploded with a thunderous boom and there was a high pitch ringing in the soldier's ears that sounded like an alarm. The whole catapult burst into flames and so were all the knights running in all different directions, screaming as loud as they could and died. Other soldiers ran to the nearest cow bath, but died of shock. Men on horses pulled the catapults with other men to follow the giant out of the castle.

Twenty fireballs flew through the air to hit Furrengee in the back until the giant made an abrupt stop; turned around, thrust his hands out in front of the fireballs that were flying at him and they stopped immediately and fired back. The fireballs flew back at the the catapults and blew them to pieces. The knights screamed in pain as they crawled away from the explosion of fire. The soldiers that were on fire or barely escaped the explosion, moved quickly to take off their armor and when they did, they peeled off their flesh with the metal armor. They cried in pain and screamed in agony inside their own pain of imprisonment.

The peasants and soldiers observing the attack had never seen a display of power like this from such an adversary. Battles were always fought with great armies, but what made this different was that it was against one man, a giant. Two knights watched the giant from a distance and realized who it was.

"This can't be who I think it is, is it?" said Sir Bombardis.

"It is," assured Sir Jenkins as he realized it was Furrengee and continued. "Wake up the king! Someone has got the mask."

"When was she taken?" asked the king as he got out of bed, rubbed his eyes and tossed the blankets aside. He enjoyed his royal sleep but disliked being woken up for insignificant things, but this took him by surprise. King Owen was upset with what happened to his daughter. They had ended the night bad and they weren't on speaking terms and now she was gone and he couldn't face her to apologize.

"She was just taken your highness," replied Sir Bombardis.

"Princess Aarilinus is the only living heir to the throne," whispered King Owen as

he tried to think who would betray him. His gut was telling him that Animus was involved, but he remembered that the Dark Wolves would have ripped his body apart.

"Assemble the rest of our knights and our five visitors! Whether they like it or not, they're going to retrieve the princess," he ordered.

"Your highness, the princes' are gone and many of the peasants are gone as well to chase after the giant. Men who aren't the ones you've selected have already left to rescue the princess," informed Sir Bombardis.

"I'm coming to join my knights to see this giant myself," ordered the king.

"There is nothing to see; it towers the castle, it has no fear for the soldiers because this giant has made diamonds out of our fireballs that have been fired at him and this giant makes the catapults explode, killing our men!" replied the knight angrily as he turned away to let the king dress.

"I must say your majesty, is it possible that the legend of Furrengee exists? That the power of love exists in a mask that unleashes unlimited power of invincibility?"

"Yes, those things are true," began the king as he remembered the past.

"I always thought of the parables as bedtime stories and never the real thing," the king lied.

"How do we stop something that's invincible?" asked Sir Bombardis.

The king paused while getting his pants on and could sense that the knight knew what was going on. The problem was that it wouldn't matter what he said now his daughter was still gone and he needed her back.

King Owen buckled his pants and put a sweater on over his shirt as he turned around to face the knight who slowly turned around to face him.

"The mask resolves around the feeling of pure love. With this power a man uses mask's power to stop anything or anyone in his path. As long as the person wearing the mask did not inflict pain on the innocent, all would be well. If the person wearing the mask was destructive or greedy, the person would be punished.

"My lord, if I may ask, if the mask resolves around love. Why send suitors to retrieve it?"

"I wanted my daughter to marry somebody who could not only protect her, but broaden the road of wealth and royalty for my family line. My wife passed away seventeen years ago and I learned that this mask worn by someone pure could bring a loved one back to life so I began sending warriors to locate and if possible retrieve it. The mask has unimaginable power of invincibility, but it also makes people around the bearer jealous and greedy that is why it is hidden."

"You didn't know where the mask was?" asked the knight.

"Not until my wife passed. I thought it was a legend or a silly story," said King Owen.

"Sir, how do you know so much about the mask, what did happen to our queen long ago?"

"A man named Adam took one of my most beautiful handmaiden without me knowing. I got her back and realized he yelled in a curse to wish the queen to die giving birth to my daughter, which happened, and that my daughter would die on her seventeenth birthday. I got angry and killed his family and took away his property. Then somehow he found the mask and took the handmaiden away and I was left with a problem of my daughter dying," replied the king as he cleared his throat after feeling a little guilty that everything was his fault.

"The legend of Furrengee goes back ten thousand years when five sorcerers ruled the land until a warrior stood up to them and their great army. A rebellion was led by this giant to free mankind against evil. A powerful wizard by the name of Xaggess joined Furrengee against the wickedness of the five sorcerers.

Furrengee and Xaggess exiled the sorcerers into an abyss to spend eternity. The balance of Ayana would be extinguished and life as we know it would be corrupt if they escaped. It has been predicted that King Animus Brokenheart would release these sorcerers and they would corrupt the land. I've only been looking out for my best interest when I heard my daughter was with a boy named Animus. It sickened me and I have no regrets for killing Animus by throwing him to the Dark Wolves. I'm hoping that they killed him without realizing who he was."

"Then Sir," began Bombardis as his eyes widened while the king nodded his head, "the Dark Wolves are the evil sorcerers and you were trying to break the curse by having the princess get married on her seventeenth birthday." King Owen looked at Bombardis and said nothing but continued to listen.

"Sir I think Adam might have found out what you did to his son and plans to kill the princess." King Owen looked at his knight suspiciously and in anger.

The Dark Wolves waited patiently after hearing the loud thunder transpiring from high above. The moment had arrived when a hole emerged from the ceiling for them to escape. Rampant looked at his fellowship, "the time has come for us to leave this prison and get our revenge!"

The Dark Wolves could hear the echos of footsteps above and the loud shakes that could only be caused by a giant and they knew it was Animus.

"It's time to depart my brothers! Come, let us be free of our captor King Owen and raise our army to cleanse the world of humans!" shouted Rampant as he led his kin through the air and left the dungeon.

The giant was in pursuit by the king's soldiers and the five princes were already on their horses together. Prince Tusk rode fast and well with Prince Domineer, Prince Lordoriouse, Prince Corsair and Prince Rubin behind him. Prince Lordoriouse and Prince Rubin had just arrived yesterday evening and met the princess at the royal ball.

Sir Norcom, Sir Voles and Sir Jenkins were hot on the trail of the giant with their torches. Hundreds of catapults were being pulled by horses and men to keep up with the speed of the giant, but were falling behind.

Furrengee walked slowly and took his time until more hot steelies fired at him. One struck him in the back of the head again and the giant turned around to see ten more were headed in his position. The soldiers fired a huge number of fireballs at once and Furrengee raised his arm up as before. He pointed his finger back at the catapults and the fireballs flew through the air then turned around to the catapults. Furrengee unleashed his curse as before and watched the fireballs hit the catapults and blew them apart. The soldiers limped away in pain from the heat while others were were burned to death. The masked giant stood for a minute and watched the soldiers cry and scream in pain from the fire and then die.

Sir Norcom trotted on his horse and saw his kin fallen to the ground and going into seizures from the pain endured. Others were screaming in agony and reaching for their helmets to pull them off, but were screaming every time they moved it because their skin was fused with the metal. Sir Voles and Sir Jenkins jumped off their horses to assist, but were stopped by Sir Norcom.

"Leave the soldiers!" ordered Sir Norcom.

"But they need us!" said Sir Voles.

"They're dead! We must pursue the giant that did this and kill him," declared Sir Norcom.

The knights rode on past the first gate until they were directly behind the giant who suddenly began to decrease in size from twenty feet to twelve feet. The stranger turned around and looked at the three knights with ten soldiers. He was carrying the princess in his arms and saw she was asleep. He walked in the woods and disappeared from sight.

Sir Norcom stopped in his tracks and raised his hand up to signal the knights to stop. There was a reason why he was holding everyone back, but Sir Voles and Sir Jenkins were beginning to get restless in their desire to catch up to Animus who looked like Furrengee.

"Why do we not go after him? We can take him," demanded Sir Voles.

"We wait for the king and the rest of the army," ordered Sir Norcom.

Suddenly, the soldiers were visited by the five princes with torches in their hands and sat on their horses. Prince Tusk led them on his black horse and looked at Sir Norcom with a sneer. He looked at the king's soldiers with a cocky smile as Prince Corsair and Prince Lordoriouse nodded politely.

"What's this? Why the wait? Let's go into the woods and slay the giant!" exclaimed Prince Tusk. "We must rescue the princess, are you cowards?"

"This creature entered the castle grounds and didn't harm any of the men. Only those that attacked him received a severe punishment. If we enter the woods we may not escape," replied Sir Norcom. "It could have a curse."

"That's ridiculous, you're nothing but a coward Sir Norcom," declared Prince Tusk.

"I think we should wait for the king," ordered Sir Norcom.

"I for one am going in there to rescue Princess Aarilinus, who's with me?" asked Prince Tusk as he pulled out his sword and raised it. Almost all the princes' raised their swords and all of King Owen's men cheered.

They all left, except Sir Norcom and Prince Rubin who stayed behind to watch them enter the woods. Prince Tusk trotted through the first group of trees and after about twenty feet he stopped. He looked around while moving his torch from side to side. The giant was nowhere to be seen and there were no tracks to be found.

Prince Tusk jumped off his horse as the other men did and walked around. There was something strange with the trees and the way they moved. There was no wind and suddenly the men began running back from the way they came in.

"The trees are alive!" exclaimed a voice.

Prince Corsair held out his sword and watched in horror as a group of trees started closing in on them. He could see their red eyes stare at them while they snarled with their big mouths and sharp teeth. The branches moved like arms and quickly attached to the soldier's limbs.

Sir Voles swung his sword at a man eating tree that was creeping towards him in a slow crawl and moved with its roots, similar to how a worm moves. Almost all the men dropped their torches out of fear as the flames burned out on the ground.

The appearance of the man eating trees was the last thing they ever expected. None of them thought about using the torches to fight the man eating trees accept Prince Corsair, Prince Lordoriouse and Prince Tusk because they hesitated to think before executing.

Prince Domineer charged at one man eating tree with his morning star and struck it as hard as he could, but he only made it angry. It charged after the prince and grabbed him with its vine like branches. Prince Domineer felt the branch wrap around his legs to pull him down and dragged him along the ground. Prince Tusk let out a yell as he sliced the tree's branches and freed his ally.

Sir Jenkins watched in horror as a screaming man was being eaten alive by a tree. It pulled the soldier into its mouth with its branches and began crushing its victim's body until the screaming ceased. Then when it was finished it smiled at Sir Jenkins and started moving towards him. Sir Voles stood next to Sir Jenkins as its branches reached them and the two fought the creature, but another man eating tree emerged from within the shadows and grabbed Sir Jenkins by his ankle. Sir Jenkins screamed as he was pulled towards the man eating tree, "help me!" he shouted.

Sir Voles watched in despair as the man eating tree shoved the knight in its mouth with his arms and hands out`. Sir Voles was held back by Prince Lordoriouse and Prince Corsair.

"Let me go, I'm going to kill it!"

The young men watched the knight scream for help while his left arm and head was sticking out of the man eating tree's mouth. Then there was one final scream before his head disappeared and they could hear that the tree's teeth had crushed the man's skull. His arm and hand slid into the tree's mouth while the crunching sound popped into their ears.

"I could have saved him!" yelled Sir Voles as he repeated over and over again. "I could have saved him!"

"Look around you fool! The trees have already devoured ten of your soldiers, we must withdraw!" ordered Prince Corsair.

Sir Voles looked around and saw a dozen man eating trees fighting over the last of the soldiers that were trying to fight them off and gave their lives.

Prince Tusk looked at his torch and then started one of the trees on fire while Prince Domineer was chopping a tree's branch with his battle axe. The trees snarled and charged after the two princes to finish them off. All of a sudden, the twelve man eating trees doubled and they enclosed in a circle around the men. Prince Lordoriouse and Corsair left Sir Voles to save Prince Tusk and Domineer. Both princes' were able to cut their kin free, but realized that they were surrounded and cut off from Sir Voles. Sir Voles turned around and screamed before he was devoured by a man eating tree. The princes' watched him scream for help, but there was nothing that they could do.

The four princes' looked at each other as they watched the trees move in and waited for death to take them. Suddenly, there was a burst of light as arrows with fire shot and struck the trees. The princes' spirits lifted as they realized they were saved.

King Owen charged through in full armor on his white horse with Sir Norcom and Prince Rubin as well as the rest of his army. The princes bowed and kneeled before King Owen.

"Your majesty," they said one after the other.

"Come, the trees are returning back to normal," commanded King Owen as the princes' called their horses and joined the king to find the princess.

Furrengee stood with Princess Aarilinus in front of him, in his arms, next to a small beautiful, waterfall that poured into a small stream. The giant was seven feet tall and he let Aarilina down to her feet. He held her gently in his muscular arms and she looked at him curiously. Her body was like a porcelain doll with the white night gown and Animus didn't want to hurt her. She looked up to the towering individual in the shiny black armor, with a cape, wearing the mask and remembered the dream of him. The princess wasn't scared anymore and looked at him with admiration. He was a mighty giant with black hair that stretched to the middle of his back. He was unlike any man she had ever seen and he nodded his head at her as though knowing who she was. Princess Aarilinus became discontent with fear after minutes of silence and the stare from his empty and dark eyes, the eyes of the mask.

Minutes of silence went by and Princess Aarilinus remembered the legend of Furrengee from father as a bedtime story. Now it seemed to be a reality to finally meet Furrengee in person, but was this real or a hoax? If it was a dream would she wake up to find herself with Prince Tusk or Domineer with ten children and a life of sadness? She thought about this for a while remembering the stories well because they were read to her by Jenna when she was eight years old. Minutes went by until she realized it was not a dream but as real as she could ever imagine.

"Who are you?" she demanded.

61

"Someone who would die for you," said a muffled voice behind the mask.

Furrengee walked towards the princess slowly and saw that she was not frightened. He put his right hand up with his index finger pointing up gesturing her to be at ease.

Carefully and slowly Furrengee placed both hands over the mask and slowly renounced it. Beautiful flashes of light illuminated over the mask and went in all different directions as it was just over his face. Instantly, Furrengee's armor vanished and his black hair retraced back to the length of his shoulders and became blonde. The mask was brought down just below the possessor's chin unmasking his identity.

Princess Aarilinus' mouth dropped as she gasped in a sound as though she was about to cry, "Animus!"

Animus smiled and felt her hug and kiss him, "Father forced me to betray you, will you ever forgive me?" she cried.

"I forgive you, I should have known he was behind it," said Animus as he took a deep breath and felt better now that he knew the truth.

The two were together; they held each other like never before with undamaged love for each other. They were made for each other and now no one could break them apart. She looked into Animus' eyes, her smile answered to a hundred wishes since the first day she laid eyes on him. He touched her back with his fingertips as they came closer to each other, exquisitely, where she touched his chest and neck with her fingernails lightly. Animus closed his eyes and smiled as her lips met with his.

"Animus," she cried emotionally as her lips trembled. "My dear Animus, you rescued me from death." she continued to cry and took a deep breath before she hugged him and then looked at the mask. "Is this the mask that Furrengee wore?" she whispered.

Animus looked at the mask that was in his right hand and turned his head to smile at Aarilina, "yes it is. With this mask we will be together with unstoppable force and rule the kingdom together."

They found a spot on the ground that was soft and they gathered leaves to make a bed and laid down together. Animus touched the princess' cheek with his hand while she looked at him. It was smooth, hard, well sculpted and she continued to smile at him.

Aarilina leaned down from sitting on his stomach to touch his lips with hers. Now they had freedom to do what they wished and no one would stand in their way.

The mask, once worn by a great warrior, helped them in more ways than possible. Aarilina laid her head upon Animus' chest and listened to his heartbeat which sent her
fears away realizing he was here in front of her.

For hours they laid and looked into each other's eyes and before they knew it the sky began to lighten up. Animus opened his eyes from taking a nap to see the sun peeking up from the horizon and the princess woke up with a smile because it wasn't a dream. They watched the sunrise as the sky displayed the start of a new day.

"Tell me you love me," she whispered and he kissed her.

After the kiss he looked at her and touched her hand, "I went through death to save you," said Animus. "What do you think?"

Aarilina looked at him ad smiled, "what is it like wearing the mask?"

"Well," replied Animus. "When I wear it, I can feel a consciousness that I have never felt before. Thousands of voices, memories, decisions made sometimes with or without my consent and sometimes before I realize it. It gives me strength to endure. It can't be used to attack or kill offensively. The spirits inside the mask would not let me attack offensively that was why I could only put a curse on those that fired on me first. The moments I stepped on the soldiers was on accident and the Fiduciaries understood that," answered Animus.

"Incredible," said Aarilina as she continued to smile.

"Your birthday is today," he said as he got up and remembered the curse that Aarilina would die on her seventeenth birthday.

Aarilina looked at him and then at the ground. Animus knew that she didn't care about her birthday and that she didn't know about the curse that she would die.

"Actually, my birthday was yesterday," began Aarilina as she watched Animus smile and closed his eyes. "Father had a ball so that I could meet the princes that would be seeking the mask for my hand in marriage. They were going to leave this morning to seek the mask."

"Well, they're probably disappointed, but I'm happy that your ok," said Animus after he re-opened his eyes and he thought about the prophecy and that she would die from a broken heart.

"Well it wasn't ok, father's been a tyrant by locking me up in the High Tower. He claims I'll die on my birthday, but I don't believe in that cow pie superstition," she said.

"I should protect you now, I'm vulnerable when I don't wear the mask. The curse on the man eating trees probably wore off when I retracted the mask from my face," replied Animus as he turned to look at the sunrise

The princess smiled as she got up from the ground and leaned up against him. She slowly rested her head on his shoulder. She imagined no day without him and knew father would try to kill him, but she would die for him. She would charge through a rain of fire for Animus before giving up her love for him

"Animus let's run away from here," Aarilina began with a shaken voice. "Run away with me, I have nothing here and I want you, I need you!"

Animus smiled and was about to pick up the mask from the tree stump until Aarilina stood in front of him. Her eyes glazed into his eyes and kissed him.

"Tell me you love me."

"You know I do," replied Animus.

"Then lets get out of here," she said.

"No, I'm going to protect you from dying on your seventeenth birthday and I will face your father with the mask."

"I already told you, my birthday was yesterday and nothing happened. Nothing is going to happen, I swear to you. I won't leave you," cried Aarilina as she realized she lied to Animus because of her thought to commit suicide before Furrengee smashed through the window to take her away.

"Something doesn't feel right," said Animus as he thought about his father's warning about the age seventeen rather than her actual birthday.

"Father will wait until the moment you take off the mask and your back is turned. Then he will kill you!" she replied.

"Aria needs you," replied Animus as he stared into her eyes.

"No it doesn't," answered Aarilina. "I've realized that before you saved me."

"The people of Aria need you. You give them hope, dreams, happiness, joy, forgiveness, justice and love," said Animus.

The princess took a deep breath and smiled while nodding her head, "ok."

Animus moved the princess aside to get the mask as he thought of King Owen. He thought about how hard he worked to get the mask with so many hardships against him. His eyes turned to the smooth metal mask forged by the warrior himself and the fiduciaries who were inside of it. Animus bent down to pick it up.

Suddenly, he was stricken with fear when an arrow had been shot and embedded itself into the hollow eye of the mask. The thought to grasp the mask soon withered in fear as he started to feel an adrenaline rush come over him.

Animus turned his head to the princess who turned to him and then back at the soldiers. The princess got up and stood in front of Animus with her left hand in his and turned her head slowly to look at him and knew he was scared.

The peasant became frustrated as his lips began trembling while looking at the tyrant who was king. They sat on horses and Animus saw the king with five men who looked important. One of them Animus recognized as the one who delivered the letter that lured him to Humming Forest. He was dressed in black armor and rode the same black stallion. The rider who gave him the letter and beat him senseless at Humming Forest was staring at him and looked like he wanted to kill him.

Animus watched the soldiers surround them and knew that if he didn't get the mask that they would be in trouble. The soldiers were armed with every weapon imaginable and were waiting for the order by the king.

The farm boy could already feel the ropes pulling his limbs apart by horses. He could feel a slight tingling sensation on the back of his neck and looked at the mask of Furrengee that was on the tree stump, just within his grasp.

Animus watched the knights slowly draw in from about a hundred feet, but then stopped when the king raised his hand to hold position at about fifty feet. The archers waited for the order of the king to fire their arrows. Animus turned his head to the princess and knew from the expression on her face that he wasn't the only one scared.

It was in this moment that Animus realized that the king would have him killed with an arrow to the heart and take the mask. The peasant took a step towards the king and could see the evil glare in his eyes.

"Not another step, peasant. I won't hesitate to have you killed," began King Owen. "You were responsible for a lot of deaths. You killed my men and made them suffer. Now I will make you suffer in agony."

"Your men fired first," said Animus. "They got what they they deserve. I was protecting the princess."

"She was in her room under my protection, idiot!" yelled King Owen.

The five princes' aimed their crossbows as Animus turned his head to the mask with the arrow stuck in its eye then back to the king.

Animus knew without the mask he would not be able to become invincible and save the princess from being killed on her birthday. Everything that he had ever known to be good would be lost. Animus remembered something that his father told him; *if no one stands up against the king then no one will.*

"You're quite a survivor farmer, I torched your home, killed your family, threw you to the Dark Wolves and you just keep turning up alive," said King Owen.

"Liar!" screamed Animus in anger.

"Yes," said King Owen with a smile realizing he hit a nerve.

"I killed your mom and your father. I skinned them alive to torture them and let your brothers watch before I set them on fire."

"I will kill you!" yelled Animus

"Then I did the same thing to your brother and sisters," laughed King Owen

"What do you think of that?" continued King Owen.

"You're not a king," yelled Animus. "You're not a man! You're a monster!"

"You've brought this upon yourself!" exclaimed King Owen.

"The laws of Aria state that no home on a claimed land will be destroyed!" yelled the peasant as he heard King Owen laugh at him with his associates.

"I am the law! You forget Animus that I'm the king and I can do whatever I want."

"Father, how could you?" screamed the princess. `

"I guess we have to compete in a new challenge since the farmer has the mask?" laughed Prince Domineer. The princess heard what the prince said and became angry.

"Do we have to get back into this topic again of why?" asked King Owen to his daughter

"Father, I told you I'm never going to marry any of the men you've chosen for me!"

"Aarilina bring the mask and come along," ordered King Owen.

"Father, please-" begged Aarilina. "Let him go."

"Pick up the mask and come along, say good-bye to Animus," said King Owen.

The soldiers got into position by stretching their bows as the five princes' got in position to shoot their crossbows into Animus' chest. Aarilina turned to Animus as she began to cry. Animus took a deep breath and watched her pick up the mask with the arrow stuck to the stump in the eye of the mask.

The princess grabbed the mask and felt its smooth metal texture and began walking slowly to her father. She felt a strong energy from the mask and the energy made the hair on the back on her neck stand up. Princess Aarilinus wondered if Animus could be looked upon by the people of Aria as a hero and be respected for being a farmer then he would be a great king. With each step she made came the voice of her mother telling her; *Aarilina save him, save Animus.*

Princess Aarilinus felt her heart flutter and turned her head to see her mother walking beside her. Aarilina looked at her father and the soldiers and she realized that they couldn't see her mother. Only she could see her mother.

The queen held Aarilina's hand that was holding the mask. With such assurance Aarilina feared nothing, not even death itself. For all things, but love comes to an end, even death ends.

Quickly, with great speed Aarilina turned around and ran as fast as she could, faster than thought possible. Prince Tusk aimed his crossbow straight at Animus and pulled the trigger, but realized it was going to hit the princess, "blast it, foolish woman!"

King Owen turned to the prince suspiciously then back at his daughter and realized what had happened and yelled, "no!"

In slow motion Princess Aarilinus watched Animus open his arms as his face expressed how overjoyed he was that she was coming back to him. Suddenly, it began to change to shock and horror at the same time. She felt something pierce her back that was sharp running next to her left shoulder blade and through her chest.

"No!" she heard Animus scream.

Blood dispersed all over her dress and she collapsed in his arms. Aarilina knew she was dying and had seconds before she would lay to rest as the words slipped through her lips as she went unconscious.

"I would die for you," she cried and closed her eyes as Animus held her in his arms. "I've always loved you and I would die for you," she repeated and then became silent.

"No Aarilina! Come back, come back to me!" he cried as he cradled her in his arms and touched her chest with the arrow sticking out of the white night gown, soaked in blood.

Flashbacks entered his mind of how hard he worked to retrieve the mask, defeat the Widow Plant, meet Furrengee and put on the mask. He felt a volcanic eruption of anger that had no end, while crying in tears for his loss. For the greatest thing in his life was gone, forever, and there was no way to bring her back. Animus looked at the king as his puffy eyes and red face revealed to the king how much he loved her.

"I'm going to have you executed!" exclaimed King Owen as he looked at Prince Tusk.

"You will do nothing, for my father will declare war against Aria and I give you my word that my country will wipe you out!"

"You fool, I will have you castrated and fed to the Dark Wolves before your father even misses you!" shouted King Owen.

"Would you like to solve our differences now!" declared Prince Tusk as he pulled out his sword.

Sir Norcom and the other knights pulled out their swords and concentrated their attention to Prince Tusk. The king shook his head in disappointment and completely understood why his daughter didn't want to marry him.

"Lay down your damn sword sir," ordered Sir Norcom slowly with intimidation

"Are you deaf?" demanded the king as he stared at Prince Tusk.

"Lay down your sword!" repeated King Owen slowly.

Prince Tusk threw his sword on the ground and turned his attention back to the king. Prince Tusk didn't expect to have the king turn against him or the knights for that matter.

"You will leave these grounds and if you ever return you will be killed," ordered King Owen.

"This is war!" declared Prince Tusk as he rode off through the woods on his stallion. The king made it clear that there would be no mistakes and his daughter would not be harmed. Prince Tusk had broken that rule and was banished from the kingdom, but it didn't matter because the damage had been done. King Owen turned his attention to Animus who had the mask in his possession and now a new problem emerged.

King Owen immediately charged with his horse to see his daughter for one last time and to be with her. Abruptly, Animus held them back with his hand and showed them the mask.

"Get back! I have the mask and I won't hesitate to use it," he screamed in anger.

King Owen halted as his horse let out a whinny with his knights and the princes did the same. It was a very crucial moment of despair, but still they wanted to proceed. King Owen wanted to be with his daughter and to hold her close, now that he lost her.

"You're bluffing!" yelled King Owen. "You're not going to put it on because you'll be killed.

"You mock me! I'll put it on and revive the man eating trees or weld your skin to your armor. I'll do it, don't think I won't!" Animus continued.

King Owen turned to the four remainder princes'. He knew what he promised them if they retrieved the mask. Now he would have to break that promise and risk losing the alliance.

"I must have you leave me in peace, I've lost my daughter and feel responsible," said the king sadly.

"You've given me the opportunity to meet the future queen," replied Corsair.

"Yes," answered the others.

"She did have a lot of qualities that other women didn't have," answered Prince Lordoriouse.

"She was a woman that didn't want to give herself to just anyone," said Lord Domineer.

"The loss of a man's daughter should be left alone to grieve on his own," said Prince Rubin.

All four Princes' nodded to King Owen and rode away. The King looked at Animus who was glaring at him and held the mask tightly in his right hand. Animus gently touched Aarilina's face with his left bloody hand. It was soaked in her blood and it shook in shock because he couldn't believe she was gone.

He was angry and wanted to kill the king. He could already picture himself choking the king with his two hands, squeezing it with all his might and watching the blood emerge in King Owen's eyes. Animus opened his eyes and stared at the king. His fingers gripped the sharp edge of the mask so hard that blood began to stream and stain the mask. The peasant exchanged hands and looked at his right hand to see the wounds on his finger tips. His wrists hurt from being so tense, but he couldn't help himself from being angry. The farm boy suddenly heard his father's voice; *The mask would not allow any offensive attack through its possession only in defense would he prevail.*

The peasant looked at his hands filled with Aarilina's blood and the new blood from his finger tips that continued to bleed. He turned the mask over to look at its face and saw stains of blood down both cheeks of the mask that looked like tears. The farm boy could feel numbness in parts of his back as the tightness started in his left hand. He began to think about what his father told him.

"Animus," began King Owen. "I meant no harm to my daughter, I loved her."

"Just as you would love to see her life spent with someone else. You tried to kill me by throwing me to the Dark Wolves and marry Aarilina to a prince who didn't deserve her!" yelled Animus.

"I'm sorry, but you can never be a king because a prophecy was foretold that if you became king, Aria would fall. A farmer can never be king, he's not smart enough to make important decisions. Peasants are stupid people that must be told what to do."

"You're a fool and you're so self absorbed that you let her die!" yelled Animus.

"Animus give me the mask if you put it on you'll be destroyed. You don't know the mask as well as I do," declared King Owen.

Animus got an idea and looked around to see the knights looking at him with fear. They were scared of him and they knew it was because he had the mask.

"You knew my father didn't you," said Animus and the king glared at him. "My father was Adam Brokenheart, the Rogue Warrior that saved my mother from you, he put a curse on your wife to die giving birth and that your only daughter would die the same age as your wife. I tried to save her and this is your fault!" exclaimed Animus as he watched the king become angry.

"I curse you old man! I'm going to put this mask on and you will know my true intentions," yelled the peasant as he put the mask on.

A burst of light struck the eyes of the knights. The soldiers who were scared fired their bows and arrows at Animus many of the soldiers threw their spears as well.

"Don't fire your weapons," shouted King Owen, but it was too late. Furrengee turned his head to the arrows that were coming to him and quickly put out his hand. The arrows stopped in mid air just before him and shot backwards to the soldiers who fired them.

Sir Norcom and King Owen watched with dismay as the soldiers fell off their horses with arrows and spears stuck in their chests. Furrengee looked down to see Aarilina's body lying on the ground. Animus who was Furrengee, pulled the arrow out of her heart. He placed his hand over the wound which healed and lifted her body up into his chest.

The king feared what the mask would do to him and knew it could be destructive. The mask started to give off its own illumination that was like lightning striking the ground. The king and his soldiers watched the display of power with amazement.

The Culminate Amethyst

The ghostly figure of Aarilina's mother appeared before Furrengee. He knew who she was and lowered Aarilina down so that the queen could see her daughter for one last time. Queen Aarilinus looked at Furrengee with a stern look and knew it was Animus wearing the mask. She gestured to have the princess on the ground and so Animus proceeded.

King Owen could see his wife and opened his mouth in shock as he choked up with tears. Queen Aarilinus kneeled down to her daughter who was on the ground and whispered her daughter's name then whispered into her ear.

Suddenly, Aarilina gasped for breath and was in shock of what was going on and opened her eyes immediately to the sight of her mother smiling. The princess thought it was amazing to see her mother because she died when Aarilina was born and the only thing that remained a memory was the dreams of meeting her.

The princess took a deep breath and turned her head to see the glowing mask. The red blood was gone and Aarilina got up from the ground and stood in front of her mother to give her a hug. Her mother looked at King Owen and nodded before smiling just as she disappeared out of thin air.

The mask's white light grew into an intense blaze. It was the emotions expressed by the mask of all the warriors who wore it in the past. Intense memories engulfed the king and minds of his knights of Animus and the princess' time together.

They could understand why the princess chose Animus and realized as king he would be courageous. The king and the soldiers realized that by having Aarilina marry someone else that she would have killed herself and Aria would've fallen into darkness. King Owen was wrong to believe Animus was unworthy.

The flashes of light stopped and Animus was still wearing the mask with armor and continued to wear it. He looked at the princess as she looked at her faithful subjects. She was healed, but still wearing the dress stained with blood. They were amazed and got off their horses as King Owen did to touch and hug her. The princess felt a tremendous push of love and Animus shook hands with the knights.

All of the soldiers were overjoyed that she was alive. King Owen ran through the crowd and picked her up from the ground and gave her a big hug.

"Will you ever find it in your heart to forgive me!" cried the king as he picked her up and held her in his arms. No monarch would have expected a son or daughter to come back to life after taking an arrow through the chest. The king set her down on the ground and looked at her as she smiled.

"Father, I would like you to meet Animus," she began as King Owen smiled at her just before Animus took off the mask and, just as before, the armor, cape, long black hair disappeared revealing Animus as he looked before.

"Knights we've got preparations to make for your future king and queen."

Animus got goose bumps after hearing those words and smiled. The power of the mask worked and now he was going to be with Aarilina.

"Father I was told by mother that love is the strongest feeling in the world. What does she mean by that?"

"It doesn't matter, what matters is that you're alive," answered her father.

The princess looked at her father and realized something had changed inside of him. He was no longer cruel with sarcasm and it seemed things would get better. King Owen turned to look at Animus, "I'm in debt to you Animus for saving my daughter's life. It seems to me that you're the best match for her."

"I don't know what to say?" replied Animus.

"Say you'll accept," smiled the king.

"Ok," smiled Animus.

The soldiers in the kingdom that were killed and injured were healed and brought back to life by Animus when he put the mask back on. That morning, preparations were made by the king for Animus to be knighted and in the afternoon he would be made king. Thousands of people witnessed the peasant kneel before King Owen as he slowly pulled out his sword, the King's Sword to be knighted. Princess Aarilinus watched father brush the sword up against the young man's two shoulders and conversed with Animus' name.

Obviously earlier the king lied about killing Animus' family and burning their house. The Brokenheart family was present at the knighting ceremony. They were all dressed in satin and silk, wearing the richest clothing to witness such a gracious event.

"Rise, Sir Animus Brokenheart," grinned King Owen as the knight rose up with the polished shiny armor.

The wind blew his long blonde hair back and he turned around to face the people he was sworn in to defend and protect. The crowds cheered and clapped their hands and the knight bowed. He felt awkward and anxious at first as he saw so many people clap their hands, but he relaxed and smiled at them.

Princess Aarilinus stepped out in the sun with Animus. She was dressed in a red, satin color dress with a gold belt and smiled at her people. The golden crown sparkled against the glimmer of the sun as they both heard the crowds clapping.

She hugged him and whispered in his ear, "I've got to go."

"Go where?" he asked with a smile.

"My handmaidens have dresses to show me and to try on," she answered as she kissed his cheek.

Animus watched her run away with a group of handmaidens through the opening of a corridor. The knight was ecstatic and couldn't wait to see her again and turned around to see his father looking at him with a smile on his face.

"Father," he said.

"I'm so proud of you," said Adam.

"Thank you, I'm still adjusting from being a nobody to a knight."

"You were never a nobody," said Adam confused and he continued. "I'm going away with your mother while your brother's and sisters stay here at the castle. I do have one question; what was it like walking around the citadel and putting on the mask?"

"It was amazing," smiled Animus. "It was everything you said it would be."

Princess Aarilinus had sent her handmaidens to the High Tower to retrieve the metal box that had her necklace. She smiled when she opened the box and pulled the Culminate Amethyst out. Her heart healed physically and mentally from her father. She knew that something had changed over her because instead of wearing it to make her father happy she was wearing it for herself and as a reminder that this was a new day. The handmaidens helped her put it on and she began to tremble that followed with a smile just as she cried and realized it became hers to wear. The Culminate Amethyst was not just a burden of loss, but a symbol of a new beginning for her life. It was the symbol of death and rebirth.

The castle was packed with people of all ages, but soon it came near for Princess Aarilinus to walk down the aisle. She was dressed in white with strings of gold, silver and blue throughout her dress. The white veil covered her face and King Owen stepped beside his daughter as they marched down the aisle.

"You look beautiful," he complimented.

"Thank you father," she whispered and smiled as she focused her eyes on Animus while imagining their first night together making sweet, patient, love.

When they arrived, King Owen conducted the vows and recited them a loud. The princess felt a strange knot in her stomach while looking into Animus' eyes and suddenly a tear fell on her left cheek. She felt like she was dreaming and would never wake up.

Minutes seemed to go forever as Animus and Aarilina listened to their vows being spoken by the king. Time seemed to stand still as they both looked into each others eyes and answered the king's questions.

The trance was broken when King Owen said, "you may kiss the bride."

Animus raised the veil over the princess' porcelain, white, face and slowly moved his head to her lips and kissed her passionately.

There was a loud cheer and clapping as they turned their heads to the crowd of people and smiled. The two marched back down the aisle, quickly, as rice was thrown at them. The doors opened and they made their way to the carriage, chased by commoners and loved ones. The carriage door closed and they rode off to the edge of the castle and stopped at a stable.

"Animus what are you doing?" asked Aarilina.

"You wanted to run away together this is our chance!" he smiled as he revealed two white stallions already saddled and ready to ride.

"Oh Animus, they're beautiful, where did you get them?"

"They were brought here as a present for you from Prince Corsair when he was here earlier."

Aarilina had no idea that Corsair was going to give her these mares and felt a little awkward accepting them.

"Oh ok," she replied.

"I'm sure he won't mind if we take them for a ride said Animus.

"Where shall we go?" she asked with a smile.

"There are some mountains overlooking the bluffs just east of here I thought by that time we could watch the sunset."

They climbed on their white stallions and charged off from the stall. The castle gates opened up and Aarilina imagined herself free as a bird. Animus felt the wind against his cheeks and knew the mask had changed their lives. They galloped for miles until they got to Shadow Mountain.

"Animus what are we doing here?" she asked.

Animus turned his head and smiled while getting off his horse. He walked over to a tree with brush and sticks and picked up the mystical weapons that helped him on his quest.

"I'm picking up my weapons that were given to me by Furrengee."

"Weapons, the legend never said that the giant had weapons," she replied.

"It doesn't matter, "he said as he fastened the magical weapons to his horse.

"You're so courageous," she smiled and they continued to ride.

When they arrived at the mountains they looked to the west and watched the sunset. Animus looked at Aarilina as the wind blew strands of hair in her face. He gently touched her chin and kissed her. From that moment, they knew they would be together forever.

The Culminate Amethyst

When "The King's Retribution" was published in 2007. There was a hundred additional pages that didn't make it in the novella. In 2006 there were two versions of the story with different scenes and because of time restraints, the shorter version of the story was what ended up being published. In 2010 the author started editing "The Culminate Amethyst and with only the climax as the original group of scenes published it in "The Legacy Anthology" in 2012. In 2018, the story was re-edited to be a regular story with different use in tone and dialogue. "The King's Retribution" had a lot of adjective and was written in a way where the words were fancy and rhymed with each other and had similarities to "Romeo and Juliet". Johnson went through each page and made the changes with action words and replaced two sentences with one sentence. The silly humor was removed as well as needless words and entire paragraph that weren't moving the story. The only sections of the story that are humorous is when the princess is asking her father about the description of the princes' and when she goes on the walk with Sir Bombardis on the royal walk where she asks him to look at her as well a take off his armor to play hide and seek. These were left in the book to stay faithful to the original concept back in 1998. The man eating trees were also put in the book, but in the original story the fight with the man eating trees goes from third person to second person. This mistake was corrected, but the author had a lot of ideas to bring in giant rock people to attack the king's soldiers as well, but this scene was not written.

There was also a ball scene that got cut from the short story and both novellas where Princess Aarilinus dances with the five princes' , but it got cut because of time restraints as well as not having the time to edit in "The Culminate Amethyst". Originally there was three scenes put together in the citadel that Animus was in, one of which was the scene of the giant snake, the Poison Widow and the Subdulox. When publishing "The King's Retribution" the author decided to only use the giant snake because there was a deadline that needed to be made. The poison Widow scene was put into "The Culminate Amethyst" and the original scenes of the giant rats and spiders were re-edited and expanded on in "The Culminate Amethyst" but when The Lord of the Rings and the Hobbit came out. The giant spiders were changed to giant tarrantulas to be more original. There was also a short scene where Aarilinus is in her room looking at the stars and praying that Animus would be ok, but this scene was ultimately cut because it conflicted with other scenes where she told him off and partly because Animus was captured and she thought he was in the citadel. Johnson added the necklace that Princess Aarilinus was wearing as an underlying theme to the story that was never there originally. The idea was that the story was about forgiving the past and moving forward to the future.

Additionally, the author has plans to unify the two novellas into one novel with all the scenes together and new scenes in one book.

Synopsis

Animus is a peasant who is in love with Princess Aarilinus and is willing to do anything for her love. Her father is king, loves his daughter even more and wants her to marry a prince who can protect her and his kingdom. Animus learns that the king has announced a contest for five men who are princes' to go into the deadly citadel to retrieve the mask of Furrengee. It is a mystical mask that makes the person who wears it invincible. The peasant talks to his father and learns more about the mask than he realizes. He finds out that that relationship between his father and the king runs deeper than a chasm.

Animus goes on the quest with a map given to him by his father and with a little bit of luck he learns that there is a prophecy about him and a deadly fate that threatens the princess. Only the mask can save them both and make things right that once were wrong.

About the Author:

Ryan Keith Johnson was born in Stillwater and grew up in Somerset. He started writing in grade school and decided to write a novel in sixth grade and completed it in junior high. In 1996 he wrote a poem called "Young, Sweetness Forever" for his grandmother in a collection of poems for a book called "Poetry Anthology for Young Americans."

In the fall of 1997, Johnson moved up to Rice Lake Wisconsin for Mechanical Design and started writing a short story that would end up becoming "The King's Retribution" and the following year of 1998 the story was expanded that followed two more short stories, "Lion Ascend" and "The Temple of the Incubus".

Johnson left Rice Lake to return home and attended Brown Institute for graphic design . He continued to write and expand on "The King's Retribution" after attending a correspondence school at Long Ridge Writer's Group. He learned the essentials of writing in scenes and creating transitions for scenes. This helped to keep the story from being wordy. He also created his own technique of creating an extended scene for the story.

The author also wrote song lyrics after he graduated high school that would later be in a book called "What I Think About You: Song Lyrics and Poetry". He started writing song lyrics in the fall of 1991 and continued through until he graduated.

Johnson is currently writing new novellas; The Demon Slayer, The Will of the Wylde, The Angel Visits and two children's books. He continues to write song lyrics and poems and is writing a group of novels.